This book belon

ROBIN

of course…

who else

[handwritten graffiti overlaying the page: "VACATION", "CAT", "OM", "MAYHEM", "OM", "AN", "Bordom BUSTER"]

Self-portrait here ↲

(You need to draw yourself.)

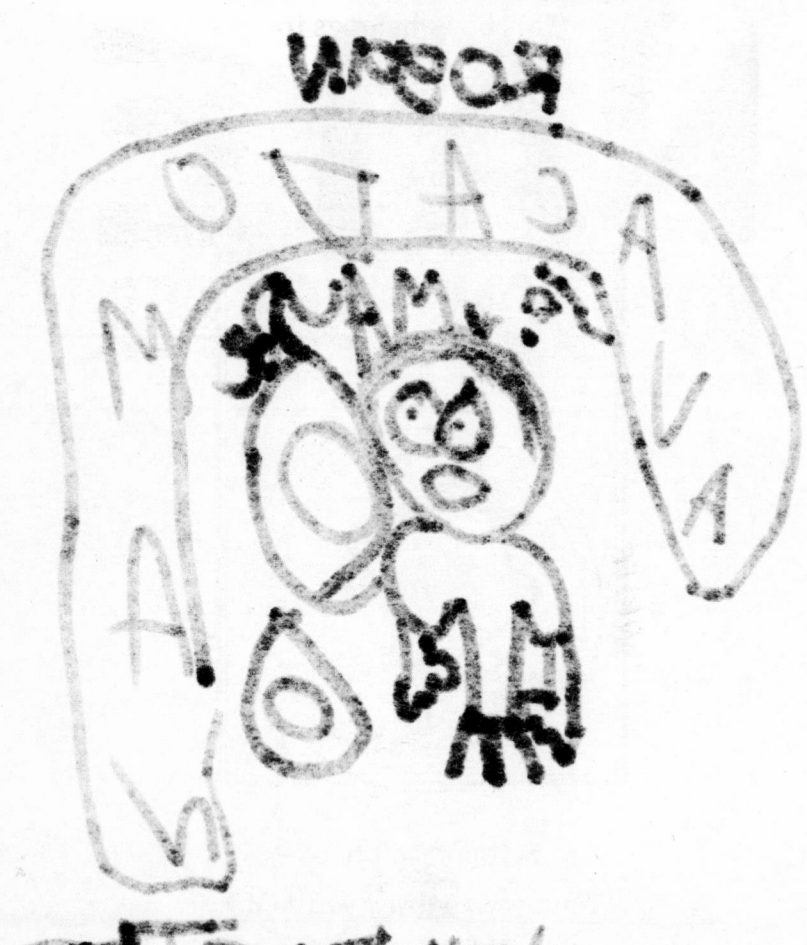

Lincoln Peirce

BiG NATE

BOREDOM BUSTER

DRAW LAUGH SCRIBBLE WRITE DRAW LAUGH SCRIBBLE WRITE

CAKE

onsie

HarperCollins *Children's Books*

First published in Great Britain by HarperCollins Children's Books 2011
HarperCollins Children's Books is a division of HarperCollinsPublishers Ltd,
77-85 Fulham Palace Road, Hammersmith, London W6 8JB

The HarperCollins Children's Books website address is
www.harpercollins.co.uk

4

Text and illustrations copyright © 2011 United Feature Syndicate, Inc

The author asserts the moral right to be identified as the author and
illustrator of this work.

ISBN: 978-0-00-743239-4
Printed and bound in England by
Clays Ltd, St Ives plc

Mixed Sources
Product group from well-managed
forests and other controlled sources
www.fsc.org   Cert no. SW-CIC-000
© 1996 Forest Stewardship Council

FSC is a non-profit international organisation established to promote the
responsible management of the world's forests. Products carrying the FSC
label are independently certified to assure consumers that they come
from forests that are managed to meet the social, economic and
ecological needs of present and future generations.

Find out more about HarperCollins and the environment at
www.harpercollins.co.uk/green

For Big Nate Fans Everywhere
Especially if you love:
Cheez Doodles,
Comics,
Fortune Cookies,
Doodling and
Detention (OK, forget that last one.)

SPOTLIGHT ON BIG NATE

Nate is awesome.
Here's why.

Nate knows he's des-tined for greatness.
Because he's no average sixth grader. He's meant for BIG things. He may not be Joe Honour Roll, but Nate's got many other more important talents.

THE MANY WAYS NATE SURPASSES ALL OTHERS:

Cartooning genius
(Speciality: teacher caricatures)

Football goalie

Table football star

Nickname tsar of P.S. 38

WHAT DO YOU THINK IS SO GREAT ABOUT NATE?

1.

2.

3.

4.

5.

6.

7.

8. Cheez Doodle–eating champ

9.

10.

AND... HERE'S
NATE'S BIGGEST
CLAIM TO FAME:
He is the <u>all-time record
holder</u> for detentions at
his school.

DOODLE DREAMS

Do you dream in doodles? Let loose and fill the page ALL OVER!

POW!

NATE'S TOP SECRET CODE

Nate is an ace at cracking codes. Maybe one day he'll become a super spy.

He invented a special code so he and his best buddies, Teddy and Francis, can send top-secret messages for their eyes only – NOT for Nate's least favourite teacher, Mrs Godfrey. Or for Gina, his Goody Two-shoes classmate, who always gets him into trouble!

CODE CHART Use this	
alphabet to decode the secret	⊞ = U
messages in this book!	⊟ = V

⊙ = A	⊓ = E	▽ = I	◑ = M	⊠ = Q	◎ = W
⊟ = B	⊠ = F	◪ = J	◣ = N	⊟ = R	⬛ = X
△ = C	⊠ = G	▣ = K	⊞ = O	◨ = S	⬛ = Y
◙ = D	▭ = H	▬ = L	⊓ = P	◆ = T	⊠ = Z

DETENTION ROOM

Watch out! Nate's in trouble AGAIN, with Godzilla... aka Mrs Godfrey.

It's up to YOU to get him out of detention. Using the letters in the word "detention," how many other words can you make? If you find 15 words, Nate's free to play football with his best friends, Teddy and Francis! For a super challenge, find 25 words.

DETENTION

1. Tent
2. Ten
3. Tin
4. Den
5. Tie
6. No
7. **dent**
8. Toe
9. note
10. net
11. Nee

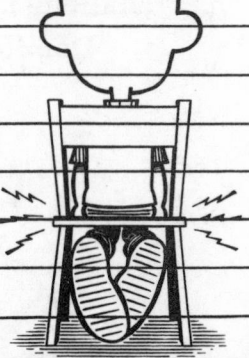

MY BUTT'S ASLEEP.

Act fast, or Nate might get stuck in detention... forever!

12.
13.

(Turn the page.)

DETENTION

14.	
15.	
16.	
17.	
18.	
19.	
20.	
21.	
22.	
23.	
24.	
25.	

Congratulations! You have won the super challenge. Now Nate gets to eat Cheez Doodles every day for a week!

YYYYYYESSS!

INVENT-A-COMIX

Bring on the laughs! BIG time. Draw the funniest scene you can think of using Ben Franklin, volleyball, and Nate!

CAST OF CHARACTERS

Nate's school, P.S. 38, may smell like mystery meat... ewww.

But it's also where Nate rules, and where you will find his best friends (#1 and #1A), his worst enemies, and his long-time crush – ever since first grade!

Can you name every character in Nate's world? Then decode the secret messages below them. Use the code chart on page 4.

Who are these characters?

Francis

Gina

Allen

teddy

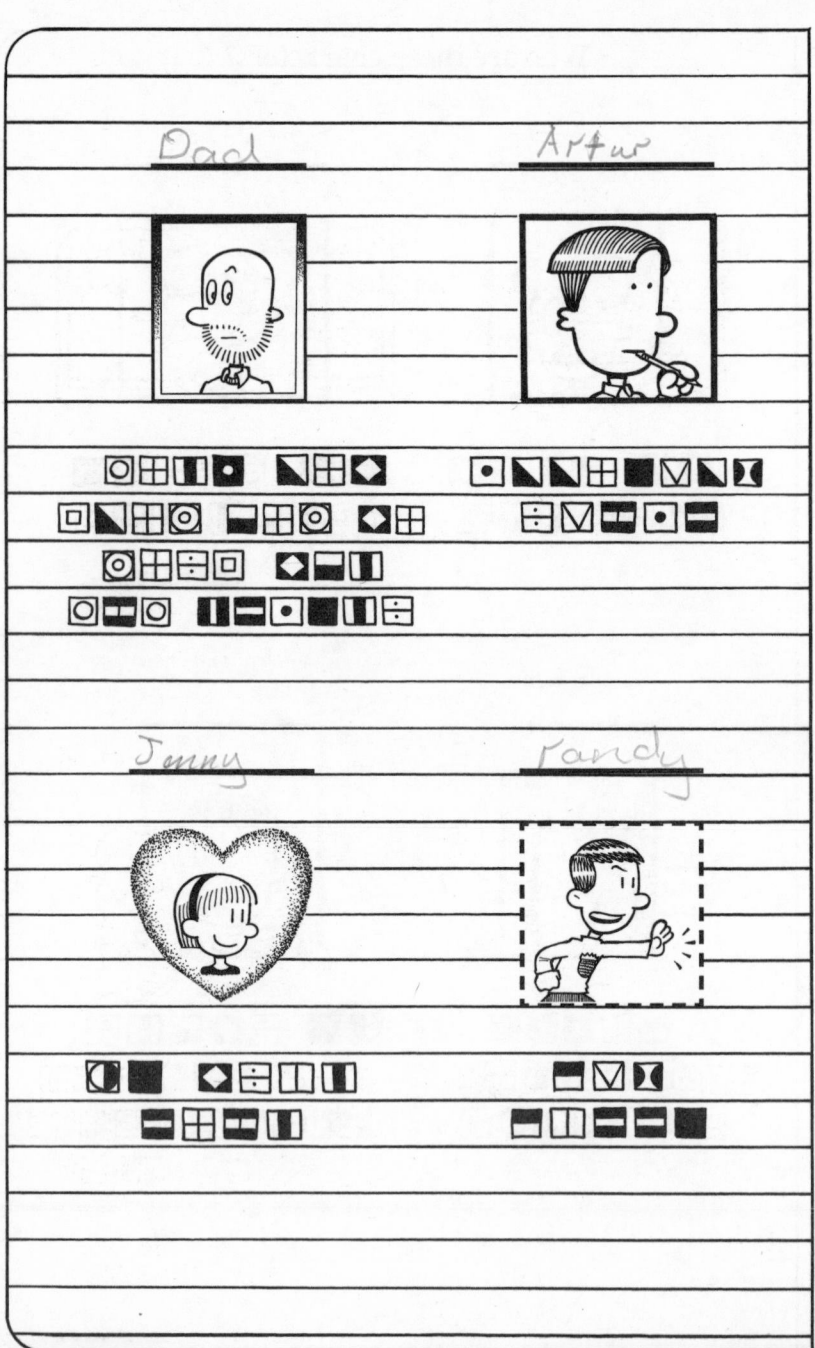

Dee Dee

spitsy

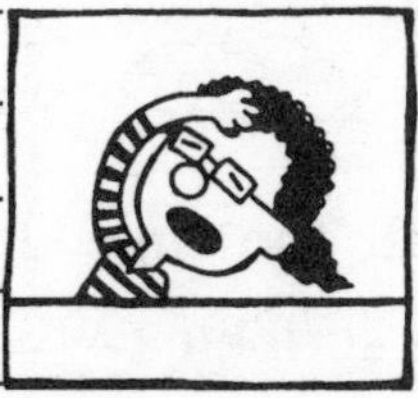

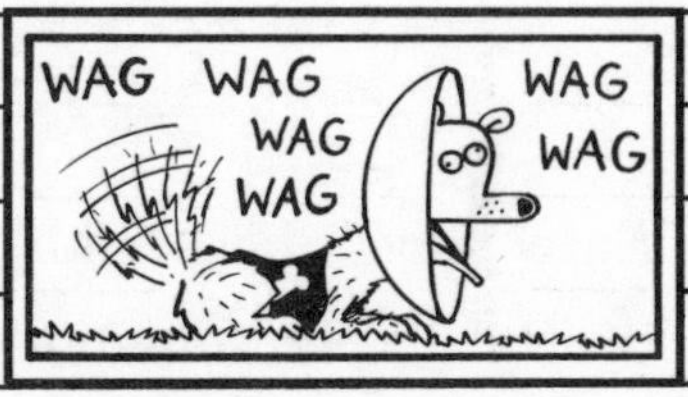

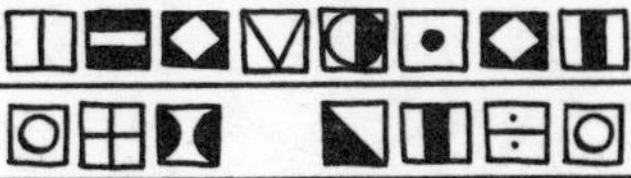

Chad

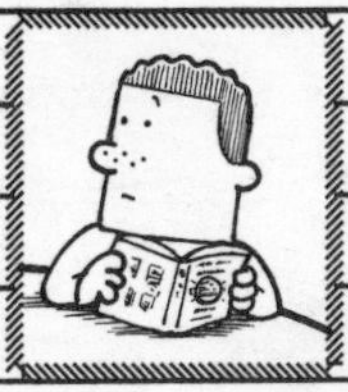

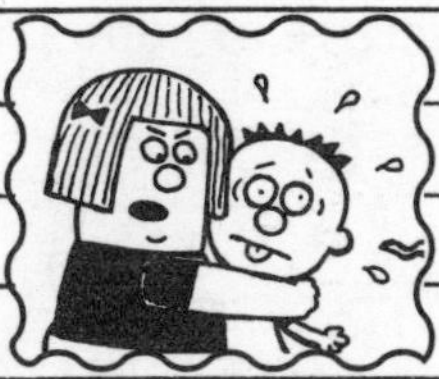

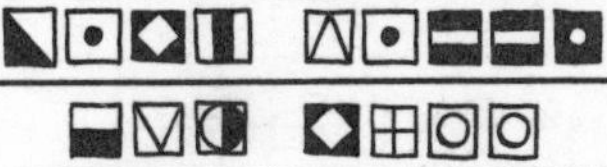

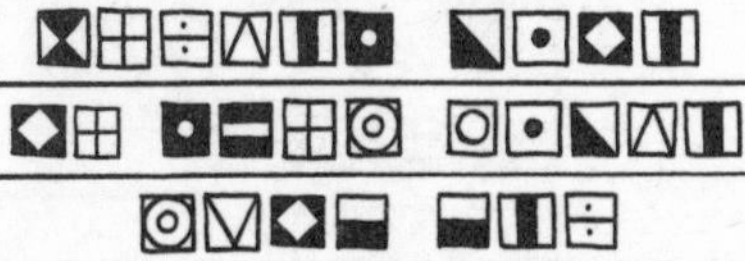

SUPER SCRIBBLE GAME

Nate plays the scribble game all the time. It's pretty simple: somebody makes a scribble…

…and then you have to turn that scribble into a picture of something.

Fight boredom – start scribbling! Play the scribble game. Turn this scribble into something super cool.

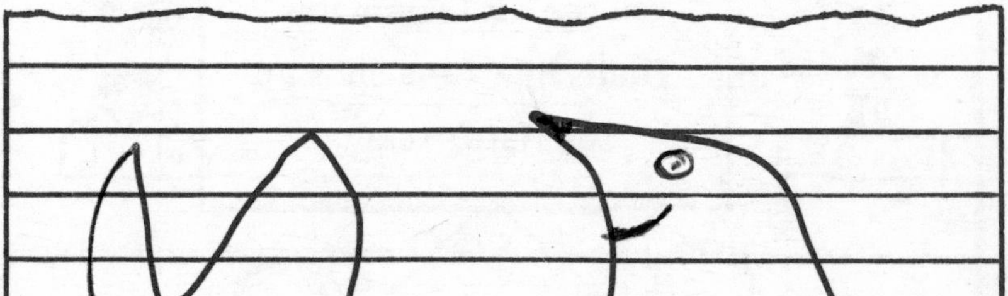

Don't forget to write a caption for it:

A seal

Here's your chance to create your own All-Star team. Who would you pick? Don't forget – YOU get to be captain.

DRAW YOURSELF HERE!

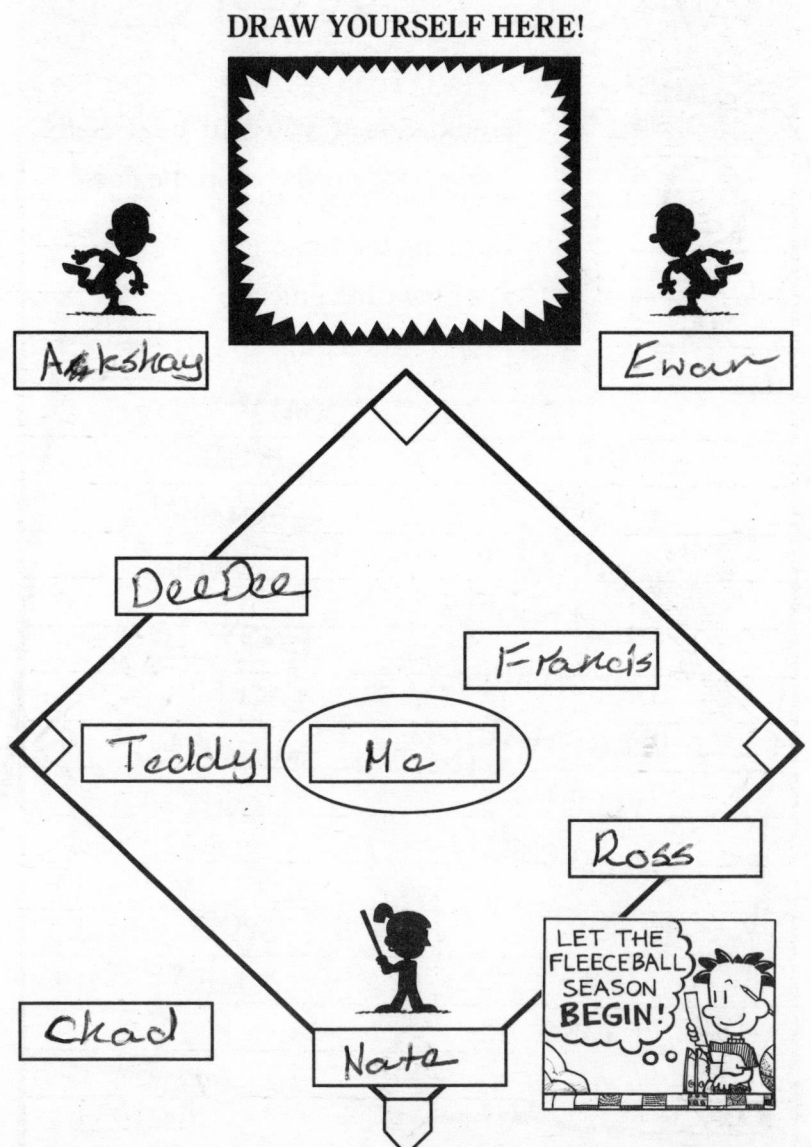

Akshay

Ewan

DeeDee

Francis

Teddy

Me

Ross

Chad

Nate

LET THE FLEECEBALL SEASON BEGIN!

NATE'S WACKY WORLD

Quick! See if you can beat Nate!
Find all 22 words before he does.

ARTIST

ARTUR

CARTOONING

CHEEZ DOODLE

DETENTION

EGG SALAD

ELLEN

FLEECEBALL

FORTUNE

FRANCIS

GINA

GOALIE

GREATNESS

GREEN BEAN

HOMEWORK

JENNY

LOCKER

MR ROSA

RANDY

SPITSY

SPOFF

TEDDY

A	H	I	I	M	S	P	O	F	F	O	T	K
N	O	T	F	R	E	K	C	O	L	O	G	R
I	M	H	R	R	S	I	C	N	A	R	F	Y
G	~~E~~	~~L~~	~~D~~	~~O~~	~~O~~	~~D~~	~~Z~~	~~E~~	~~E~~	~~H~~	~~C~~	E
N	W	N	L	S	N	A	A	A	G	A	L	Y
Z	O	F	I	A	S	J	T	C	R	L	E	D
N	R	O	R	P	B	N	E	T	E	T	N	N
R	K	R	I	N	E	E	O	N	E	O	U	A
A	R	T	I	S	T	O	C	I	N	D	E	R
E	S	U	S	T	N	Y	K	E	B	Y	D	O
Y	O	N	O	I	T	N	E	T	E	D	W	Y
F	G	E	N	O	E	G	G	S	A	L	A	D
N	T	G	O	A	L	I	E	F	N	R	F	D

POETRY SLAM: RHYME TIME

When inspiration strikes, it's time to write! The *Wright* way! Nate Wright, that is. Can you write an ode to your favourite snack?

ODE TO A CHEEZ DOODLE by Nate Wright

I search the grocery store in haste,

To find that sweet lip-smacking taste.

And there it is, in aisle nine.

It's just a dollar thirty-nine!

A bag of Doodles most delicious.

Check the label: they're nutritious!

And do you know how satisfied

I feel while munching Doodles fried?

I savour each bright orange curl,

Until it seems I just might hurl.

Their praises I will always sing.

Cheez Doodles are my everything.

Is it ice cream? Or pizza? Or Cheez Doodles, Nate's true love? What makes YOU drool with hunger? Write it here: _____

Make a list of words that describe or are related to your yummy treat.

Example: pizza (crispy, cheese, cheesy, pepperoni, crust, sauce, bubbly, gooey)

P⊛ETRY! 9OЯTFOLIO!
Nate Wright

You can be a poet, too. Put your skills to the test!
Here are some words that rhyme with **funny**:
sunny, money, honey

Now you try! Come up with words that rhyme
with **Nate: great, late, wait** *fate, mate*

Tree: bee, sea, me, glee
Come up with five more! *glee, tree, pea*

Rain: mane, lane, drain, cane
List six more! *Tame, Frame, game,*
Shame, train, grain

Now try these:
Crash *bash*
Hot *not*
Spit *fit*
Game *lame*
Mind *kind*

Duh.

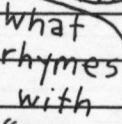

what rhymes with "Duh"?

Now try writing couplets (that's
two lines that rhyme).

MANY   JENNY
PENNY   ANY

☺ Some say ketchup is not a food
Well, I say they are really rude.

☺ When I feel a rumble in my tummy,
I search frantically for something ___yummy___.

☺ Nothing in the world is more special to me
Than syrup from a maple ___tree___!

☺ When a bag of marshmallows is near,
You can see me grinning from ear to ___ear___.

Write your own couplets here:

Now you are ready to write an ode. Remember, the last word in each line of a couplet has to rhyme.

ODE TO _____

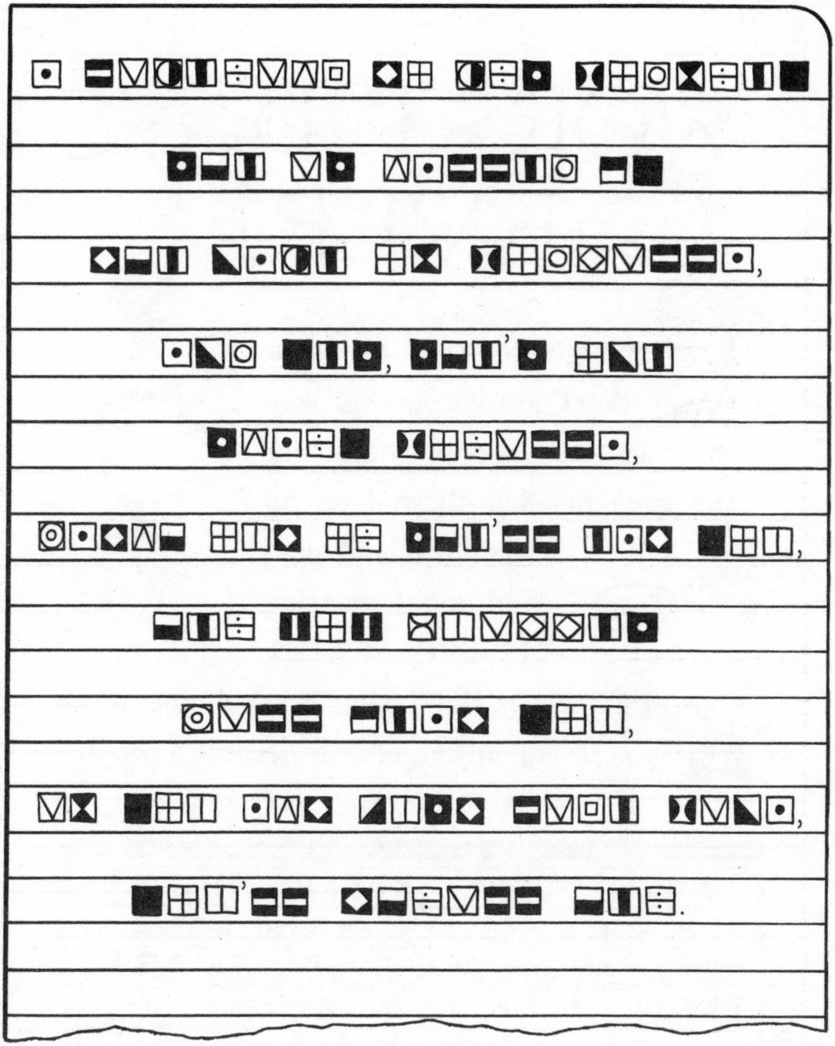

WORST DAYS EVER!

Even though Nate is awesome, things don't always go his way. He's had his share of bad days. Like the time his dad showed up for middle school skating night wearing FIGURE SKATES. Or the Spring Fever dance, when Jenny and Artur became a couple.

MIDDLE SCHOOL SKATING NIGHT
The entire sixth grade was there... *INCLUDING PARENTS!* Result: total humiliation.

WHEE!

Hey, NATE! LOVE your Dad's FIGURE SKATES!!

HA HA HA HA HA

Have you ever had a bad day? What if your list of WORST DAYS EVER looked like this? Would you rank them as BAD, AWFUL, or WORST?

WORST DAYS EVER

1. On your way to a birthday party, a bird poops on you.

☑ BAD   ☐ AWFUL   ☐ WORST

2. On picture day, you spill ketchup on your sweater.

☐ BAD   ☑ AWFUL   ☐ WORST

3. Your teacher gives you a pop quiz.

☑ BAD   ☐ AWFUL   ☐ WORST

4. You wear your shirt backwards to school.

☐ BAD   ☑ AWFUL   ☐ WORST

5. You lose your lucky charm.

☐ BAD   ☐ AWFUL   ☑ WORST

6. Everyone thinks you wet your pants.

☐ BAD   ☐ AWFUL   ☑ WORST

7. You forgot to do all your homework.
   □ BAD   □ AWFUL   ☑ WORST

8. You throw up in front of your crush.
   □ BAD   ☑ AWFUL   □ WORST

9. Your best friend moves away.
   □ BAD   □ AWFUL   ☑ WORST

10. Your sister ate all the Cheez Doodles.
    □ BAD   □ AWFUL   ☑ WORST

11. You just got detention.
    □ BAD   ☑ AWFUL   □ WORST

POP QUIZ!

Nate's never been the teacher's pet. That's
because he's too busy being the class clown!
Can you name Nate's teachers?
Match the teachers to the classes they teach.

MATHS

GYM

SOCIAL STUDIES

SCIENCE

ENGLISH

ART

QUESTION
OF THE DAY:

HOW MANY TEACHERS DOES IT TAKE TO SCREW IN A LIGHTBULB?

COOL COMIX!

Nate's bossy big sister, Ellen, is annoying him... again! Fill in the speech bubbles and help him get his revenge.

BEST BUDS

Nate, Teddy, Francis and Spitsy love to hang out. Make sure they're all together! Can you figure out who should go where so that each character appears only once in every row, column, and box of four squares?

N = **NATE**

F = **FRANCIS**

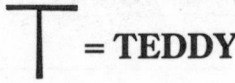

T = **TEDDY**

S = **SPITSY**

NICKNAME TSAR

Nate gets called a lot of things... like...

Actually, Nate is the master of inventing nick-names for other people, like his scary social studies teacher, Mrs Godfrey. Help Nate come up with the rest of his list. Now you are a nickname tsar, just like Nate!

CHECK MY LIST!

GODFREY NICKNAMES

1. Godzilla
2. Boring.com
3. Gassy Mcgee
4. God Fried
5. Weight Crusher
6. McFatty
7.
8.
9.
10.
11.
12.
13.
14.
15.
16.

FRANCIS'S FANTASTIC SECRET ALPHABET

Francis is seriously smart! He's such a brainiac that Nate's always spying on him to find out what homework they have. It's payback time! Francis is going to fool Nate in a BIG way. He's invented a secret alphabet that Nate will never decode!

Use the alphabet to translate Francis's message to you. Don't tell Nate! You're <u>undercover</u>.

A	B	C	D	E	F	G	H	I	J	K	L	M
13	7	26	25	8	16	3	1	20	4	12	23	18

N	O	P	Q	R	S	T	U	V	W	X	Y	Z
21	11	2	15	14	24	6	10	19	22	17	9	5

$\overline{20}\ \overline{21}$ $\overline{7}\ \overline{20}\ \overline{3}$ $\overline{21}\ \overline{13}\ \overline{6}\ \overline{8}$

$\overline{11}\ \overline{21}$ $\overline{13}$ $\overline{14}\ \overline{11}\ \overline{23}\ \overline{23}$,

$\overline{23}\ \overline{11}\ \overline{11}\ \overline{12}$ $\overline{11}\ \overline{10}\ \overline{6}$ $\overline{16}\ \overline{11}\ \overline{14}$

$\overline{2}\ \overline{8}\ \overline{6}\ \overline{8}\ \overline{14}$ $\overline{2}\ \overline{13}\ \overline{21}$,

$\overline{6}\ \overline{20}\ \overline{18}\ \overline{7}\ \overline{8}\ \overline{14}$ $\overline{24}\ \overline{26}\ \overline{11}\ \overline{10}\ \overline{6}\ \overline{24}$,

$\overline{13}\ \overline{21}\ \overline{25}$ $\overline{25}\ \overline{8}\ \overline{6}\ \overline{8}\ \overline{21}\ \overline{6}\ \overline{20}\ \overline{11}\ \overline{21}$,

$\overline{11}\ \overline{16}$ $\overline{26}\ \overline{11}\ \overline{10}\ \overline{14}\ \overline{24}\ \overline{8}$.

SUPERHERO POWERS

IF YOU WERE A SUPERHERO, WHAT AMAZING POWERS WOULD YOU HAVE?

Circle your top 5!

Walking on Water	
X-ray Vision	
(Flight)	
Super Speed	
(Shape-Shifting)	
Power Hearing	
Thought Control	
(Anti-Ageing)	
Cloning	
Shrinking	
Fireproof	
(Time Travel)	

Super Jumping

Weather Master

Scaling Tall Buildings

(Mind Reading)

Breathing Under Water

Invisibility

Anti-Gravity

Force Field Generator

Magnetism

CAN YOU THINK OF ANY

OTHER SUPERPOWERS?

ADD THEM HERE:

WHAT DOES YOUR SUPERHERO DO?

SHOW YOUR SUPERHERO:

SCALING TALL BUILDINGS

CLONING

SHAPE-SHIFTING

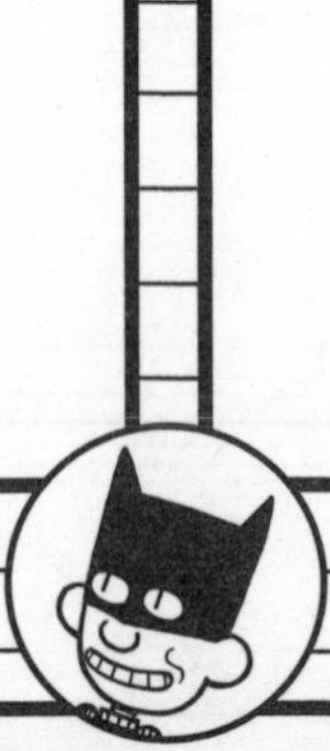

WALKING ON WATER

Does your superhero save the day?
Make your own comix.
Your name here

IN THE CAFETORIUM

Which foods gross you out? See if you can solve this crossword and name all the foods that make Nate and his friends gag!

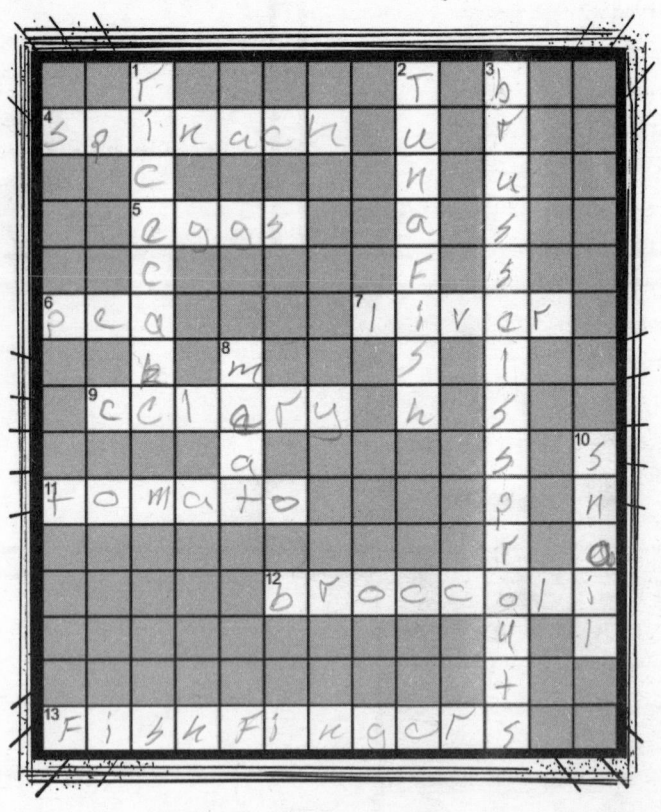

NARF
NARF
NUMF

CLUES

SLOPF
SLURP
SLOP

ACROSS

4. It's leafy and green, and Popeye eats it to grow strong! (7)

5. Chickens lay these. (4)

6. Split ___ soup. (3)

7. Rhymes with "shiver" and served with onions. (5)

9. Healthy, stringy and light green. WAY better with peanut butter. (6)

11. Red, round and rhymes with potato – if you have an American accent like Nate. (6)

12. Looks like a mini tree. Nate's dad serves it with cheese sauce. Gross. (8)

13. First word rhymes with "dish", and swims. Second word rhymes with "lingers". (4, 7)

DOWN

1. This crispy snack looks like polystyrene. Nate's dad gave them out for Halloween – ugh! (8)

2. Smelly, comes from the sea. Your mum likes to mix it with mayonnaise for sandwiches. (4, 4)

3. Round, small and green, and look like little cabbages. Yuck! (8, 7)

8. Rhymes with "feet". Dark red and slimy. (4)

10. Lives in a shell. If you were French, you'd gobble it up! (5)

THE CHAMP

Nate is the CHAMP! Solve the maze so there can be a SPOFFY in his future.

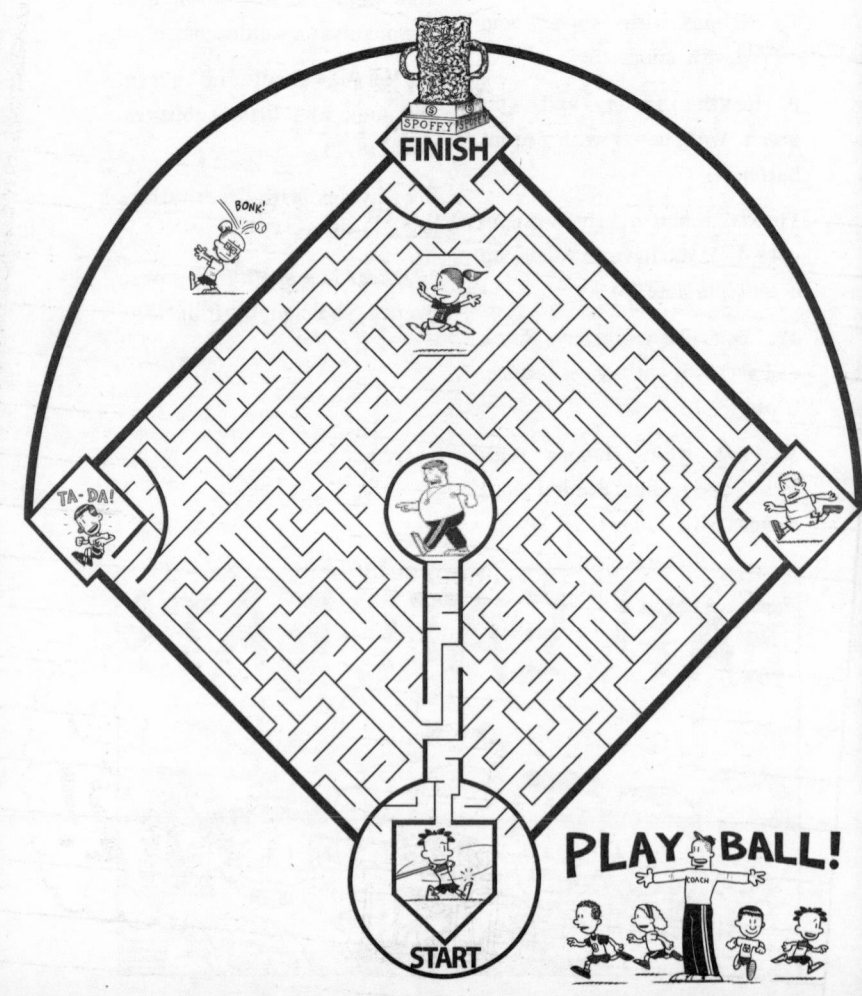

PERSONALITY POP QUIZ

WHICH BIG NATE CHARACTER ARE YOU MOST LIKE?

1. What is the snack you eat most often?

   a. Granola bar

   b. An apple

   c. Chinese food

   d. Cheez Doodles

   e. Chocolate

2. Your favourite school subject is:

   a. Social studies

   b. All of them!

   c. Gym

   d. Art

   e. English

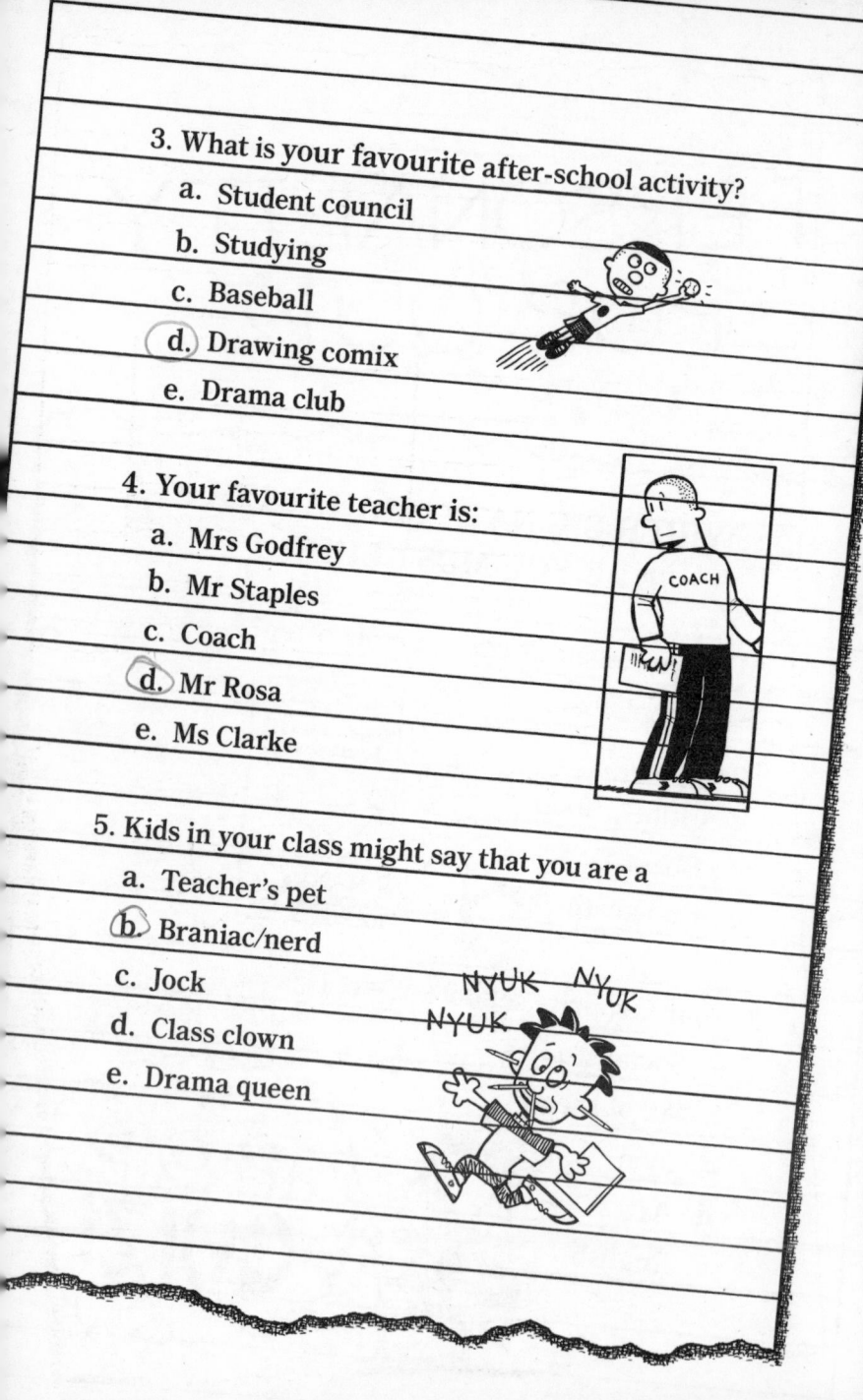

3. What is your favourite after-school activity?

   a. Student council

   b. Studying

   c. Baseball

   (d.) Drawing comix

   e. Drama club

4. Your favourite teacher is:

   a. Mrs Godfrey

   b. Mr Staples

   c. Coach

   (d.) Mr Rosa

   e. Ms Clarke

5. Kids in your class might say that you are a

   a. Teacher's pet

   (b.) Braniac/nerd

   c. Jock

   d. Class clown

   e. Drama queen

*If you answered A the most times, you're a lot like Gina. ◯

B = Francis

C = Teddy

D = Nate ②

E = Ellen

SUPER SCRIBBLE
GAME

**What can you turn
this scribble into?**

Write your caption here:

DAD IS NOT
A BLAST

DAD FACTS:

1. Nate's dad has
   been known to
   wear figure skates.   Ⓣ F

2. Nate's dad always has potato chips
   in the house.   T Ⓕ

3. Nate's dad gave out rice cakes for
   Halloween once.   Ⓣ F

4. Nate's dad is best friends with Gina's   T Ⓕ
   dad.

GENIUS

Even though Nate is a self-described genius, he does NOT plan on achieving greatness in:

Synchronised swimming

Opera

Writing a health food cookbook

CAT GROOMING

What about you? Circle all that apply!

I WON'T ACHIEVE GREATNESS IN...

Counting paper clips

Fly swatting

Speed blinking

Colour-coding my sock collection ~ Maybe

Candle-making

Underwater basket-weaving

WHAT ELSE?

LIST YOUR NON-GOALS HERE!

Never Losig

WEH

SUPERHERO COMIX

Nate created his very own superhero… Ultra-Nate.

DRAW YOURSELF AS A SUPERHERO!

CHEEZ DOODLE ALERT

Nate needs Cheez Doodles.
Help him get to them, pronto!

ANOTHER TEST!

DO YOU THINK THESE STATEMENTS ARE TRUE OR FALSE?

1. Nate's never been to detention.
   - ☐ TRUE
   - ☑ FALSE ✓

2. The earth goes around the sun. ✓
   - ☑ TRUE
   - ☐ FALSE

> IF YOU DO THIS POORLY ON THE **NEXT** TEST, NATE, YOU COULD VERY WELL END UP IN **SUMMER SCHOOL**!

3. Jenny has always loved Nate.
   - ☐ TRUE
   - ☑ FALSE ✓

4. Ben Franklin got an A in seventh grade science. ✓
   - ☐ TRUE
   - ☑ FALSE

5. Nate's neighbour's dog, Spitsy, eats his own poop. ✓
   - ☑ TRUE
   - ☐ FALSE

6. "Enslave the Mollusk" is the name of Nate's band. ✓
   - ☑ TRUE
   - ☐ FALSE

7. Pluto is a planet.
   □ TRUE   ☑ FALSE ✓

8. Nate once ran through gym class with his shorts filled with green jelly.
   □ TRUE   ☑ FALSE ✓

9. Green beans are Nate's favourite snack.
   □ TRUE   ☑ FALSE ✓

10. Nate's big sister, Ellen, was in Mrs Godfrey's class.
   ☑ TRUE   □ FALSE ✓

EXTRA CREDIT
11. "Epidermis" is another word for skin.
   □ TRUE   ☑ FALSE ✗

EXTRA EXTRA CREDIT
12. Gina once sang a duet with Nate. ✓
   □ TRUE   ☑ FALSE

$\frac{11}{12}$

TEDDY'S TOP SECRET CODE

Teddy is a sports nut. He collects sports facts and sends them to Nate. Using Teddy's secret code, help Nate decipher Teddy's amazing sports trivia.

A	B	C	D	E	F	G	H	I	J	K	L	M
Z	Y	X	W	V	U	T	S	R	Q	P	O	N

N	O	P	Q	R	S	T	U	V	W	X	Y	Z
M	L	K	J	I	H	G	F	E	D	C	B	A

58

```
___  ___ ___ ___ ___ ___ ___ ___
 Z O O   N O Y   F N K R I V H

___ ___ ___ ___   ___ ___ ___ ___   ___ ___ ___ ___ ___
 N F H G   D V Z I   Y O Z X P

___ ___ ___ ___ ___ ___ ___ ___ ___   ___ ___ ___ ___ ___
 F M W V I D V Z I   D S R O V

___ ___   ___ ___ ___   ___ ___ ___ !
 L M   G S V   Q L Y !


___ ___ ___   ___ ___ ___ ___ ___ ___ ___
 G S V   G Z O O V H G

___ ___ ___ ___ ___ ___   ___ ___   ___ ___ ___
 K O Z B V I   R M   G S V

___ ___ ___   ___ ___   ___ ___ ___ ___ ___ ___ ___ ___ ___
 M Y Z   R H   X F I I V M G O B

___ ___ ___   ___ ___ ___ ___ .
 B Z L   N R M T .
```

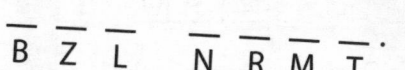

```
___ ___   ___ ___
 S V   R H
```

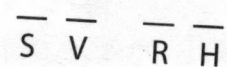

```
___ ___ ___ ___ ___   ___ ___ ___ ___ ,
 H V E V M   U V V G ,

___ ___ ___   ___ ___ ___ ___ ___ ___ .
 H R C   R M X S V H .
```

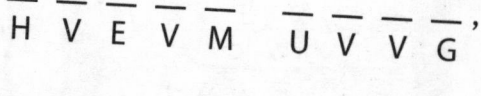

IT'S CRAZY
IN **3010**!

In Nate's Cool Comix, Ben Franklin travels from the 1700s to the 21st century in his very own time machine! If you could travel to the future, what would you find there? Use the following steps to create your time travel adventure!

First, let's review. What is a noun?

OOH! A noun is a person, place, or thing.

EXAMPLES: Nate (person), P.S. 38 (place), report card (thing)

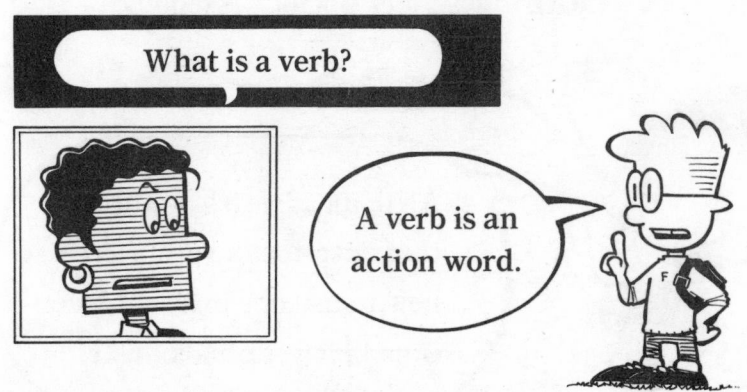

What is a verb?

A verb is an action word.

EXAMPLES: study, laugh, play, calculate

BING!

An adjective is a word that describes a noun.
Some examples of adjectives are:
AWESOME (describes me)
BORING (describes social studies)
CRAZY (describes Doctor Cesspool)

AND, an adverb is a word that describes a verb. Here's how to use one in a sentence:
Gina behaves obnoxiously.

MAKE A LIST OF THE SILLIEST
WORDS YOU CAN THINK OF:

1. Noun: Poop
2. Noun: Table
3. Noun (plural): Fire
4. Noun (plural): bright
5. Noun (plural): Oil
6. Adjective: Ahsome
7. Adjective: Great
8. Adjective: Terrible
9. Adjective: Horrid
10. Noun (plural): Pencil
11. Noun (plural): Spaghetti
12. Verb: Pump
13. Verb: laughed
14. Adjective: Cool

ANYBODY GOT
A TISSUE?

NOW TURN THE PAGE AND USE YOUR LIST
TO FILL IN THE BLANKS!

63

THE FUTURE IS WILD!

IMAGINE YOUR TIME MACHINE
LANDED IN 3010…

I've just arrived in the city ___2008___ on the

planet ___table___ , where there are lots of funny-

looking ___Fire___ that breathe ___right___

and like to eat ___oil___ . The sky is ___Ahsome___

and the water is ___Great___ . The people are

___terrible___ and ___Horrid___ . They fly these

tiny ___pencils___ and sleep on ___Spaghetti___ They

___pump___ and ___laughed___ at me instead of

saying hi. What a ___Cool___ place!

◆■□▯ ⊠▯◆▯▤▮ ▽▫
▷▫●▬▭▽▧▨ ▪⊞▯!

_____

_____

DRAW-A-THON

Nate's favourite class in school is art... it's gotta be the ONE place where Nate hasn't gotten a detention slip!

OOPS!

Never mind.

Dare to draw! Are you an artist like Nate? Or his rival, Artur? Take off your shoe and draw it!

CHECK OUT ARTUR'S DRAWING!

"OLD SHOE" BY ARTUR

TEACHER TROUBLE

Find out which teachers gave Nate detention today! Fill in the blanks so each teacher appears only once in every row, column, and box.

G = MRS GODFREY

C = COACH JOHN

P = PRINCIPAL NICHOLS

S = MR STAPLES

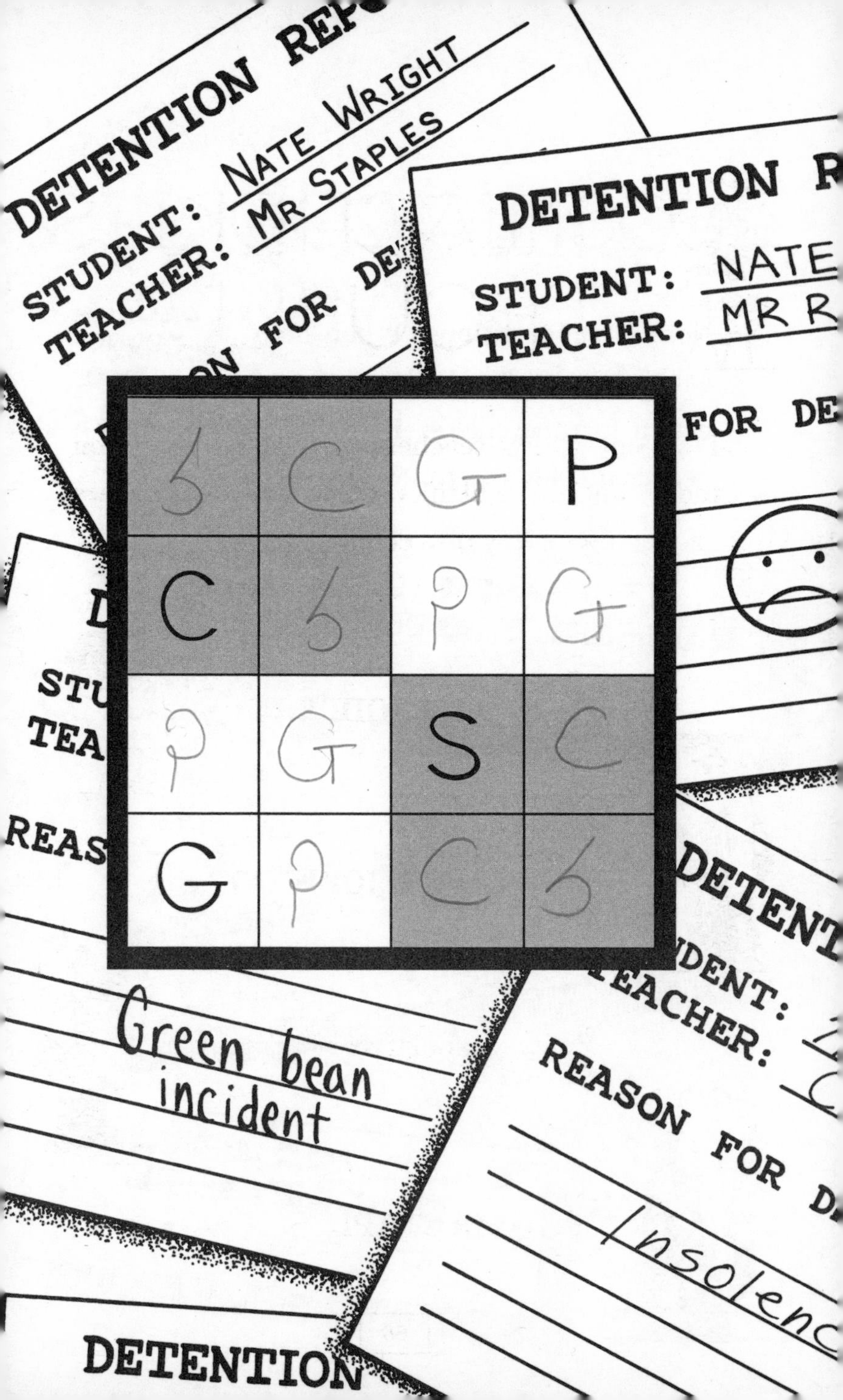

DETENTION REP...

STUDENT: NATE WRIGHT
TEACHER: MR STAPLES

...ON FOR DE...

DETENTION R

STUDENT: NATE
TEACHER: MR R

FOR DE

D

STU
TEA

REAS

6	C	G	P
C	6	P	G
P	G	S	C
G	P	C	6

DETENT

...DENT:
...EACHER:

REASON FOR D

Green bean
incident

DETENTION

REASON FOR D

Insolen...

COSMIC COOKIES

Nate is superstitious. When he eats at Pu Pu Panda, he always gets a fortune cookie. Help him decode all of his fortunes.

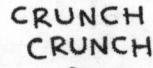

PLUS, THE COOKIES TASTE LIKE STYROFOAM.

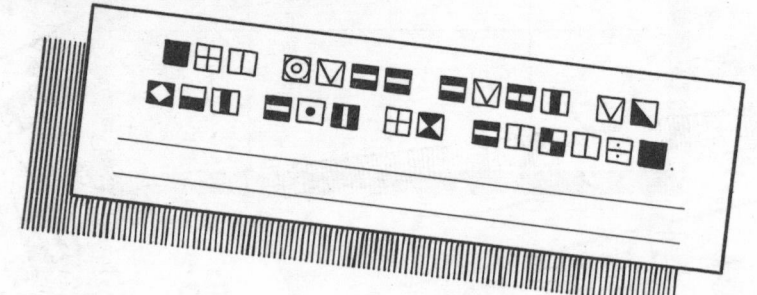

HMMMM...

Crack open a cookie... what would you want your fortune to be?

A large life is a series of small events.

Today you will surpass all others.

Hair today, gone tomorrow.

Some fortunes are so mysterious…

…**they make no sense at all!**

Make up the wackiest and weirdest fortunes ever.

WEIRD BUT TRUE

Use Francis's undercover alphabet on page 39 to decode!

```
 __  __  __     __  __  __  __  __
  6   1   8     6  20   6  13  21

__  __  __  __  __  __     __  __  __     __  __  __  __
 7   8   8   6  23   8    26  13  21     3  14  11  22

        __  __     __  __  __  __  __  __  __
        10   2      6  11   8  20   3   1   6

__  __  __  __     __  __     __  __     __  __  __  __  __
20  21  26   1      8  24    20  21    23   8  21   3   6   1 .
```

ÜBER-AWESOME WAY-OUT NAME-A-THON

Mix and match these words to make your own wacky names!

Pepperoni
Poodle
Stinky
Pumpy
Egg salad
Secret
Funky
Turbospeed
Brainiac
Royal
Giant

Crazy
Cheese
Horse
Spittle
Squid
Green bean
Poopy
Slinky
Dorkosaurus
Porcupine
Dancing

Head
King
Noogie
Machine
Smelly
Cookie
Star
Champion
Hair
Princess
Genius

HERE ARE SOME VERY SILLY NAMES:

Stinky Cheese Head

Noogie Poodle

Green Bean Funky Hair

NOW CREATE YOUR OWN!

_____ _____ _____

_____ _____

_____ _____ _____

_____ _____ _____

_____ _____

_____ _____

_____ _____ _____

_____ _____

_____ _____ _____

_____ _____ _____

_____ _____ _____

EXTRA! EXTRA!

Nate writes for the school newspaper. You can, too!

What do you see in each picture? Fill in the caption!

SUPER SCRIBBLE GAME

Guess what? It's time for the scribble game!

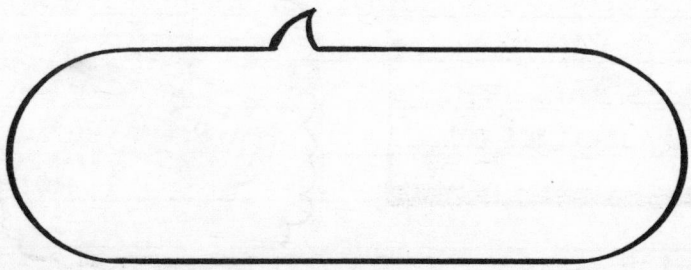

Don't forget to write a caption for your scribble!

HOLIDAYS ARE BEST!

Do you love the summer holidays as much as Nate? No teachers! No books!

LIST YOUR TOP 10 SUMMER FUN TIMES:

1.

2.

3.

4.

5.

6.

7.

8.

9.

10.

CRAZY COMIX!

**What is that wacky doctor up to? You decide.
Write your own speech bubbles.**

DOCTOR CESSPOOL!

TRASHED!

Randy has a date… with a coconut yogurt pie.

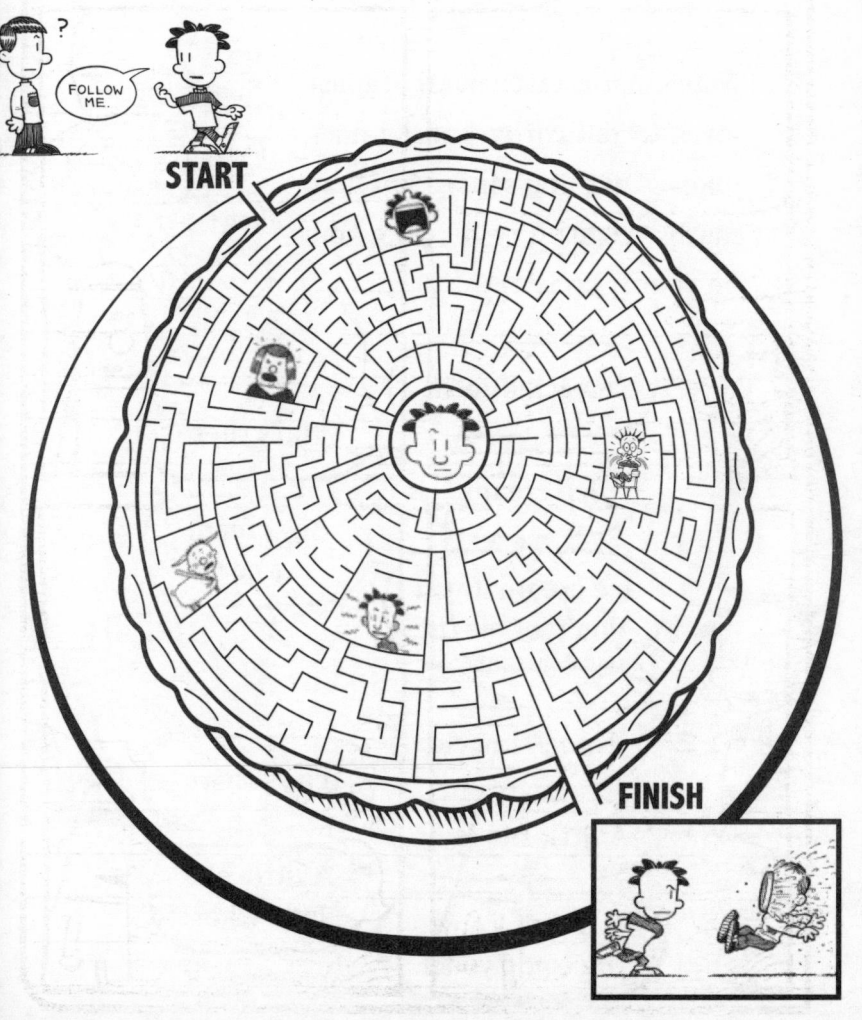

KNOCKOUT KNOCK-KNOCK JOKES

Nate's maths teacher, Mr Staples, loves to tell corny knock-knock jokes. Anything's more fun than maths, right? Try his jokes out on your friends!

Knock knock!

Who's there?

Woo.

Woo who?

Don't get so excited, it's just a joke!

Knock knock!

Who's there?

Ice cream!

Ice cream who?

Ice cream if you don't let me in!

Knock knock!

Who's there?

A little old lady.

A little old lady who?

I didn't know you could yodel.

MAKE YOUR OWN KNOCKOUT KNOCK-KNOCK JOKES!

Knock knock!

Who's there?

Ketchup!

Ketchup who?

Ketchup to me and I'll tell you.

Knock knock!

Who's there?

Police!

_____ who?

Police _____.

Knock knock!

_____ ?

Water!

_____ who?

Water _____.

Knock knock!

_____ ?

_____ !

_____ who?

_____ .

NATE CAN'T ☹ STAND IT! ☹

These are the things that get under Nate's skin.
Help him rank them from #1 to #10.

School picture day

Being sick during
the weekend

cats

"Oldies" music

Gina

Paper cuts

Egg salad

Social studies

Bubble gum that
loses its flavour
in twenty seconds

Figure skating

THINGS I CAN'T STAND!

by:  ← ~~Nate Wright, esq.~~

1. ~~Dog's finishing cabs~~
2. Sandy Shoes
3. Needles
4.
5.
6.
7.
8.
9.
10.

THE GANG'S ALL HERE!

It's a BIG NATE reunion! Fill in the blanks so each of your favourite (or LEAST favourite) BIG NATE characters appears only once in every row, column and box.

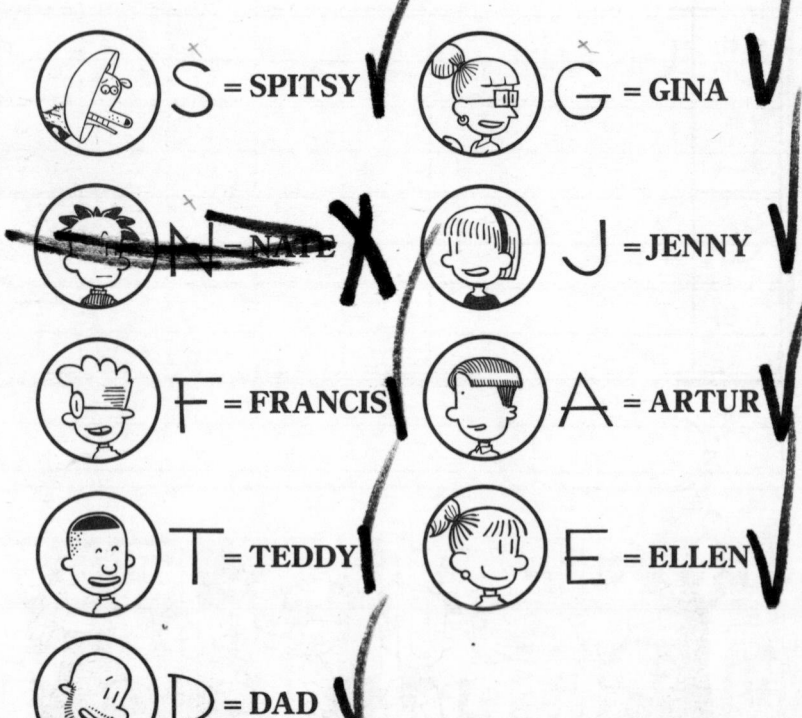

S = SPITSY

G = GINA

N = NATE

J = JENNY

F = FRANCIS

A = ARTUR

T = TEDDY

E = ELLEN

D = DAD

S	O	G	G	y	b	o	i	e
F	T	T	J		G		A	D
N	A		F	J	D	S		G
A	J	o	o	g	H	e	N	o
T	E	S	N	D	J		G	O
D	G	N	u	t	e	L	a	k
E			G		A	J		N
G	N	D	J		S		F	A
	F	i	n	e		i	S	T

COMIX BY U!

Unleash the cartoonist in you! Make your own comic using Gina, Nate, and his locker.

OK, HOLD IT. DON'T MOVE.

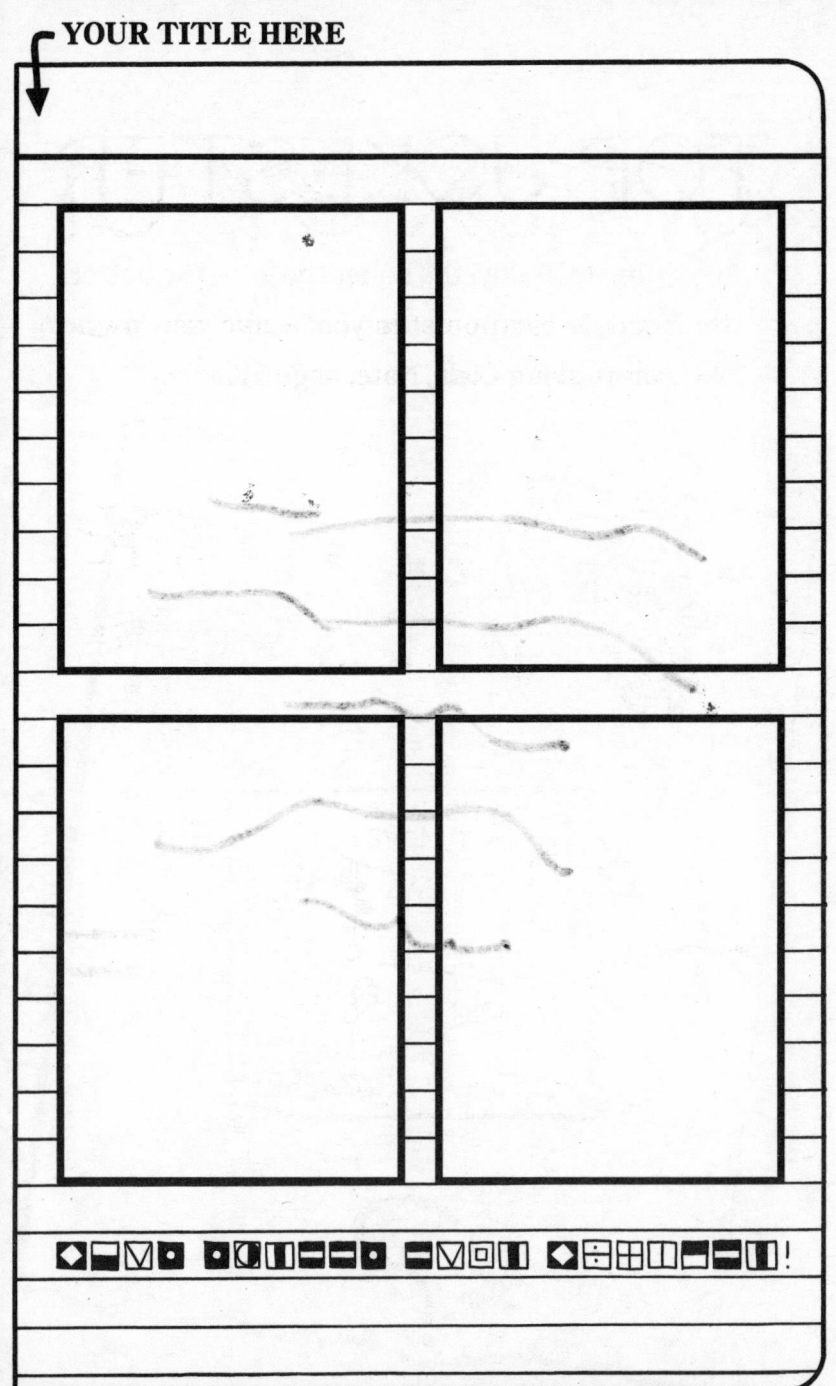

YOUR TITLE HERE

TOP JOKESTER

According to Teddy, the lamer the joke, the better! Use Teddy's totally covert code and see if the joke's on you! For code, go to page 58.

Q: $\frac{}{D} \frac{}{S} \frac{}{Z} \frac{}{Z} \frac{}{S} \frac{}{Z} \frac{}{H} \frac{}{G} \frac{}{D} \frac{}{L}$

$\frac{}{S} \frac{}{Z} \frac{}{M} \frac{}{W} \frac{}{H} \frac{}{Y} \frac{}{F} \frac{}{G}$

$\frac{}{X} \frac{}{Z} \frac{}{M} \frac{}{G} \frac{}{X} \frac{}{O} \frac{}{Z} \frac{}{K}$?

A: $\frac{}{Z} \frac{}{X} \frac{}{O} \frac{}{L} \frac{}{X} \frac{}{P}$!

DREAM SCHEME

What if you were Miss or Mister Lucky? What if you won the lottery or became a movie star and everyone wanted your autograph? Rank your top 5 all-time dreams!

MY TOP 5 ALL-TIME DREAMS:
1.
2.
3.
4.
5.

MISS OR MISTER *LUCKY!*

WHAT IS YOUR FAN SAYING?

WHAT IS YOUR MOVIE DIRECTOR SAYING?

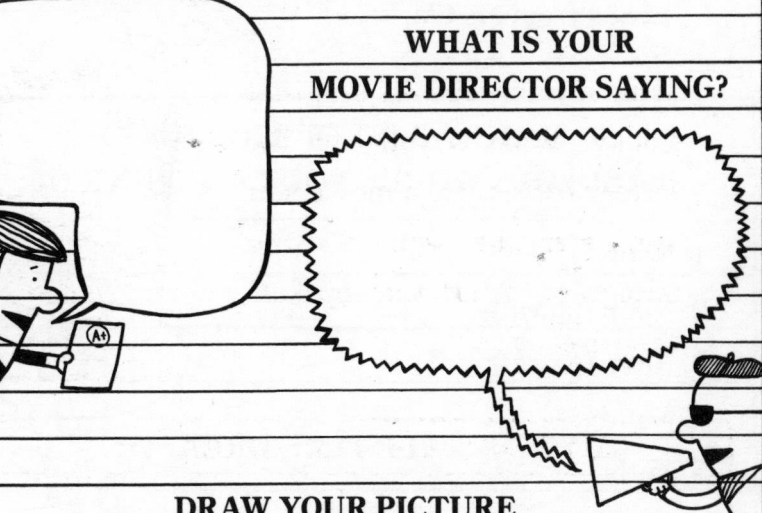

DRAW YOUR PICTURE HERE ↓

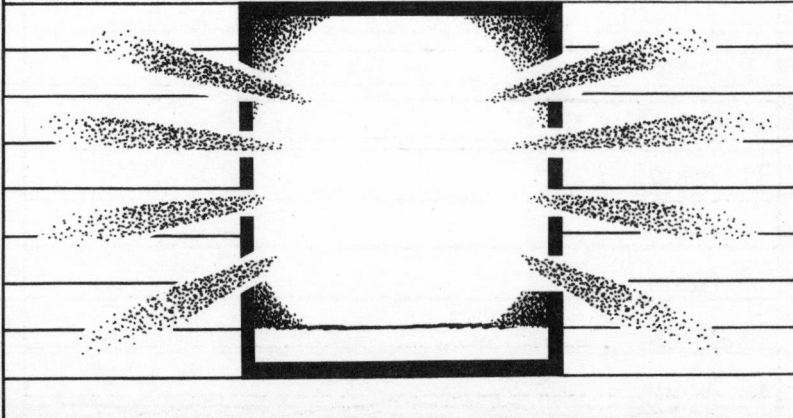

CELEBRITY CRAZE

Check out pages 61–62 for a thrilling grammar lesson from Ms Clarke!

MAKE A LIST OF THE MOST FABULOUS WORDS YOU CAN THINK OF:

1. Noun: Author
2. Noun (plural): Clothes
3. Noun (plural): Glasses
4. Noun: Greece
5. Verb: Cheer
6. Adverb: Crazily
7. Verb: ~~Leave~~ enter places
8. Adverb: Quietly
9. Verb: laugh
10. Noun: Joke-cry
11. Noun: Mini Cooper
12. Noun: rest
13. Noun: pool
14. Noun: Loch Ness
15. Noun: Home

YOU'RE A CELEBRITY!

NOW USE YOUR LIST
TO FILL IN THE BLANKS!

I Am the Greatest!

One day I'll become a famous ___Author___ .
                                    1.
I'll wear lots of ___Clothes___ and ___glasses___, and
                        2.   3.
travel to ___Greece___ every week. My fans will
                4.
___Cheer___ ___Crazily___ and shout to me!
      5.   6.
When I ___enter___ ___Quietly___, everyone
            7. Places   8.
will ___laugh___ as I dazzle the crowd. After
          9.
my ___Joke___ , I will race away in my
         10.
___Mini Cooper___ . Finally, I can take a ___rest___
      11.   12.
in a twenty-five-acre ___pool___ that over-
                          13.
looks the breathtaking ___Loch Ness___, the place
                            14.
I call ___Home___ .
          15.

NOW **THAT'S** GREATNESS!

GUESS WHAT?

How big is your brain? Using Francis's alphabet (page 39), decode these weird and wacky facts.

$\overline{13}$ $\overline{2}$ $\overline{9}$ $\overline{6}$ $\overline{1}$ $\overline{11}$ $\overline{21}$ $\overline{20}$ $\overline{21}$

$\overline{13}$ $\overline{10}$ $\overline{24}$ $\overline{6}$ $\overline{14}$ $\overline{13}$ $\overline{23}$ $\overline{20}$ $\overline{13}$

$\overline{11}$ $\overline{21}$ $\overline{26}$ $\overline{8}$ $\overline{24}$ $\overline{22}$ $\overline{13}$ $\overline{23}$ $\overline{23}$ $\overline{11}$ $\overline{22}$ $\overline{8}$ $\overline{25}$

$\overline{16}$ $\overline{11}$ $\overline{10}$ $\overline{14}$ $\overline{3}$ $\overline{11}$ $\overline{23}$ $\overline{16}$ $\overline{7}$ $\overline{13}$ $\overline{23}$ $\overline{23}$ $\overline{24}$.

__ __ __ __ __ __ __ __ __
18 11 21 12 8 9 24 20 21

__ __ __ __ __ __ __ __ __ __ __
6 1 13 20 23 13 21 25 13 14 8

__ __ __ __ __ __ __
6 14 13 20 21 8 25

__ __ __ __ __ __
6 11 2 20 26 12

__ __ __ __ __ __ __ __
26 11 26 11 21 10 6 24 .

MRS GODFREY'S
ESSAY QUESTIONS
ARE SO
INVIGORATING!

__ __ __ __   __ __ __ __ __ __
20 21 2 8 14 10 2 8 11 2 23 8

__ __ __   __ __ __ __ __   __ __ __ __ __ __ __
13 6 8 26 1 20 23 20 2 8 2 2 8 14 24

__ __   __ __ __ __   __ __   __ __ __
13 24 23 11 21 3 13 24 24 20 17

__ __ __ __ __ __ __ __
6 1 11 10 24 13 21 25

__ __ __ __ __   __ __ __
9 8 13 14 24 13 3 11 .

TRUE-LIFE COMIX

Have you ever imagined your life in cartoons? Nate has! Help create Nate's true-life story by filling in the speech bubbles.

ULTRA-NATE'S COMIX HEROES

Nate wants to become a famous cartoonist some day! He even created his own comic, "The Wacky Adventures of Doctor Cesspool." Can you find all 20 of the cartooning heroes and villains below in the super search on the next page?

ARCH~~efs~~

~~F~~ATMAN

CATWOMAN

CHARLIE BROWN

FANTASTIC ~~FOUR~~

~~GARFIELD~~

INCREDIBLE ~~HULK~~

IRON MAN

LEX LUTHOR

LINUS

~~PUFY~~

MARMA~~bude~~

PO~~poye~~

~~S~~OOPY

SPIDER-MAN

SUPERMAN

THE JOKER

WOLVERINE

WONDER WOMAN

X-MEN

```
E O A E M R A R E W Y B C T F
W T E T Y P O O N S E A H F K
O D A H N E K U D A M R A M X
L L E E S U P E R M A N R R L
V E N J F I E O Y W T E L L O
E I R O N M A N P A H N I N R
R F K K A E M N S R K A E B M
I R L E X L U T H O R M B A E
N A M R E D I P S C X O R T B
E G T I R C E I H M R W O M N
X A U E F E L I N M O T W A S
I L W O N D E R W O M A N N U
K L U H E L B I D E R C N I N
A R E C E U I H C D W N L N I
X A I A Y A A O E P M H L A L
```

"Doctor Cesspool" by Nate

BETTER THAN BEST BONE-CRUSHING TEAM NAMES

Nate's super psyched! Coach names him captain of his fleeceball team. Now Nate needs an awesome team name. Can you help him?

Potential TEAM NAMES

- Wooden runners
- Wrecking Balls
- Fire ball
- Brooms of Steel
- Kraka-Pow
- Bone-Crushers
- Ball Killers
- Wood burn
- Kerr-Orious
- Nate-orious

POW!

NAB!

THIS IS THE TEAM MASCOT!

THESE ARE THE TEAM COLOURS:

THIS IS THE TEAM CHANT:

Watch out! Gina, the know-it-all, has her own ideas. Help Gina come up with names like these:

TUG
TUG

GINA's TEAM NAMES

- ⚾ Warm & Fuzzies
- ⚾ Kuddle Kittens
- ⚾ United We Stand
- ⚾ Cuties
- ⚾ Outstanding Owls
- ⚾
- ⚾
- ⚾
- ⚾
- ⚾
- ⚾
- ⚾
- ⚾
- ⚾
- ⚾
- ⚾

THIS IS KUDDLES! MY OLDEST AND MOST FAVOUR-ITE STUFFED ANIMAL!

SHE'S PUFFY, JUST LIKE A FLEECEBALL! SEE?

DOODLE MANIA!

Does your notebook look like Nate's? Do you scribble your crush's name or design your dream car? Dare to DOODLE!

THE FORTU-NA-TOR

Can Nate make his fortune come true?

SAVED BY THE BELL

Did you hear the bell? School's out! Nate has lots of cool after-school fun – football, scout meetings, creating comix, and drumming in his band! How about you?

TOP 5 THINGS FOR AFTER-SCHOOL FUN:

1.

2.

3.

4.

5.

Find all 20 after-school activities in this super word scramble and move to the head of the class!

ACTING

BALLET

BAND

BASEBALL

BASKETBALL

CHEERLEADING

CHOIR

FRISBEE

HOCKEY

ICE-SKATING

KARATE

KICKBALL

PAINTING

PIANO

PING-PONG

POTTERY

READING

SCHOOL PAPER

TAP DANCING

VIDEO GAMES

N G Y A T E I R H G S I C L O
O N R L J T I O N E C G N L T
U I E Q K O C I P E D F W A L
P D T I H K T H S N F N P B E
X A T C E N X K A Q R D V K E
L E O Y I P A B Q E A O I C B
L L P A E T I M P N K M D I S
A R P T I V M A C M R P E K I
B E U N A T P I N U J J O R R
E E G U E L N H P O V K G E F
S H S L O G S G N I T C A A N
A C L O G N O P G N I P M D I
B A H A E T A R A K W W E I A
B C L L A B T E K S A B S N B
S T R N B O B A Q M L Z A G C

RRRRINNNGG!!

NATE! TODAY AFTER SCHOOL WILL BE **FUN**, YES?

HM?

TRASH

DETENTION CONVENTION

Where there's Nate, there's trouble. His middle name is mischief. Just kidding! (Nate does not have a middle name.)

Nate is no stranger to the detention room. Do you ever get in trouble?

Or do you get gold stars like Gina, the honour roll student?

TOP 5 TIMES YOU'VE BEEN IN TROUBLE:
(UH-OH!)

1.

2.

3.

4.

5.

TOP 5 GOLD STAR MOMENTS:

1.

2.

3.

4.

5.

EXCLAMATION GAME

Things don't always go your way just because you're awesome. You decide what Nate's saying or thinking – fill in the bubbles!

WHOA! WHAT IS NATE SAYING?

UH-OH!

YIKES!

HONOUR ROLL, OR NOT?

Gina may be a triple-A student.
But DETENTION is awaiting her!

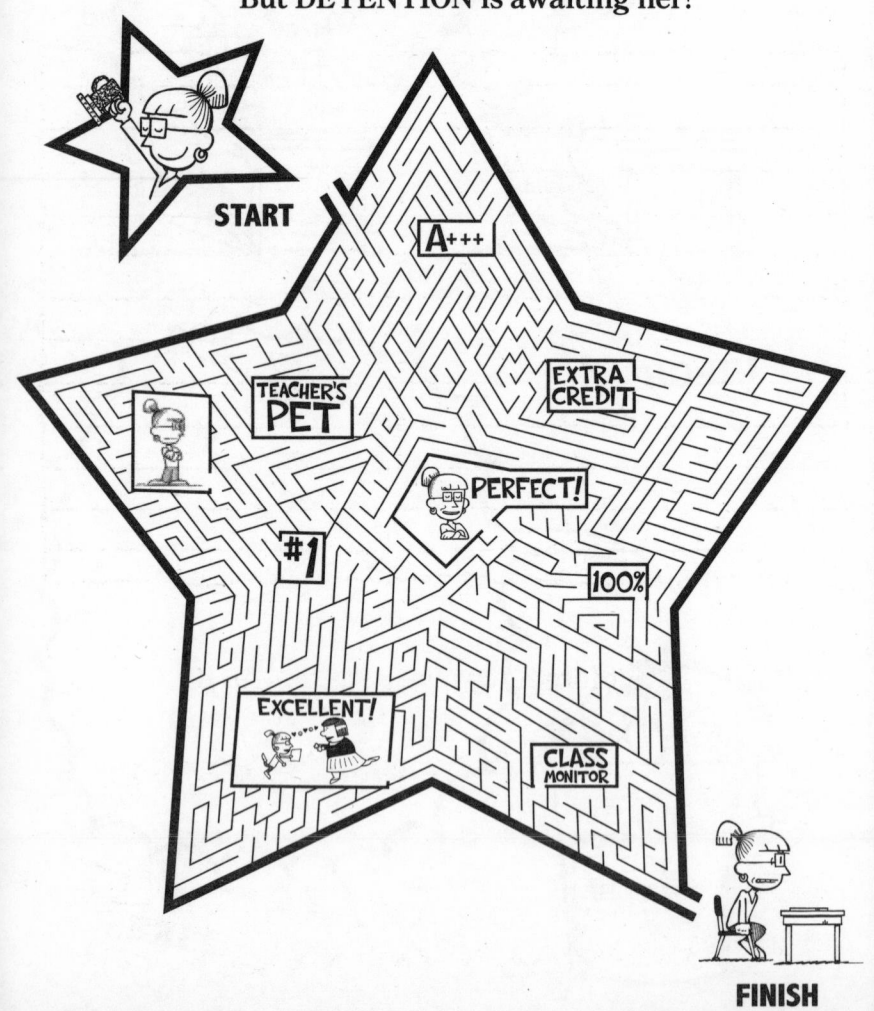

SUPER SCRIBBLE GAME

This scribble is going to turn into… what?

Don't forget to write a caption for it!

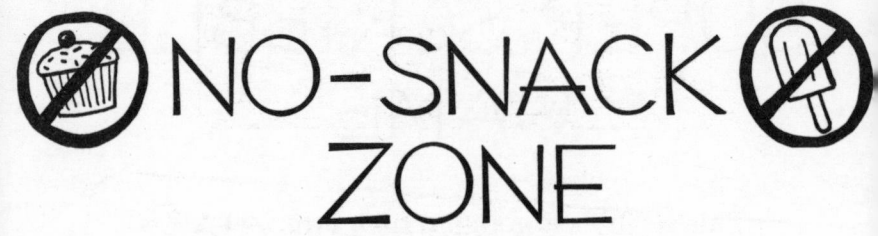

NO-SNACK ZONE

Does your school cafeteria stink like egg salad?
Eww, gross!

HERE ARE SOME OF THE FOODS NATE HATES!

Prunes

Egg salad

Squishy bananas

LIST YOUR TOP 10 WORST FOODS EVER!

1.

2.

3.

4.

5.

6.

GULP!

7.

8.

9.

10.

YOUR TRUE-LIFE STORY

You are a cartoonist. Here's your chance to draw YOUR true-life story.

I PLAY _nothing_. I HAVE A PET _Koala_.

(sport or instrument)	**(real or imaginary)**

MY BEST FRIEND	**MY FAVOURITE FOOD**

I LIVE IN _Scotland_. I ALWAYS WEAR _glasses_.

MY FAVOURITE BOOK

MY FAVOURITE MOVIE

Harry Potter Loooo

HOW'S THE GRAPHIC NOVEL COMING ALONG?

GOOD. I'M WRITING ABOUT WHAT HAPPENED IN THE THIRD INNING.

WAIT A MINUTE! YOU STRUCK OUT IN THE THIRD INNING!

YEAH. SO?

ACCORDING TO **THIS**, YOU HIT A 3-RUN **HOMER**!

I'M JUST MAKING THE STORY-LINE MORE INTERESTING.

...AND THEN YOU SAVED A KID IN THE BLEACHERS FROM **CHOK-ING** ON A **HOT DOG**??

IT'S CALLED "ARTISTIC LICENCE."

© 2009 by NEA, Inc.

TRIVIA TEST!

How well do you know Big Nate?
It's time to test your Nate Knowledge!

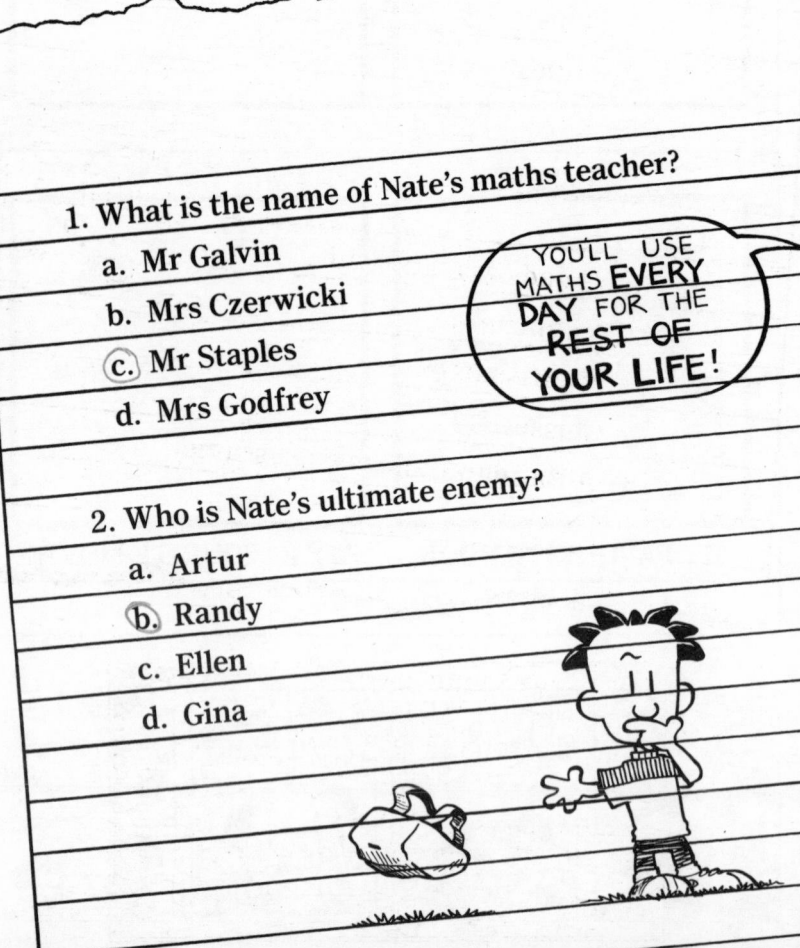

1. What is the name of Nate's maths teacher?

a. Mr Galvin

b. Mrs Czerwicki

c. Mr Staples

d. Mrs Godfrey

YOU'LL USE MATHS **EVERY DAY** FOR THE ~~REST OF~~ **YOUR LIFE**!

2. Who is Nate's ultimate enemy?

a. Artur

b. Randy

c. Ellen

d. Gina

3. What is Nate's most favourite food?

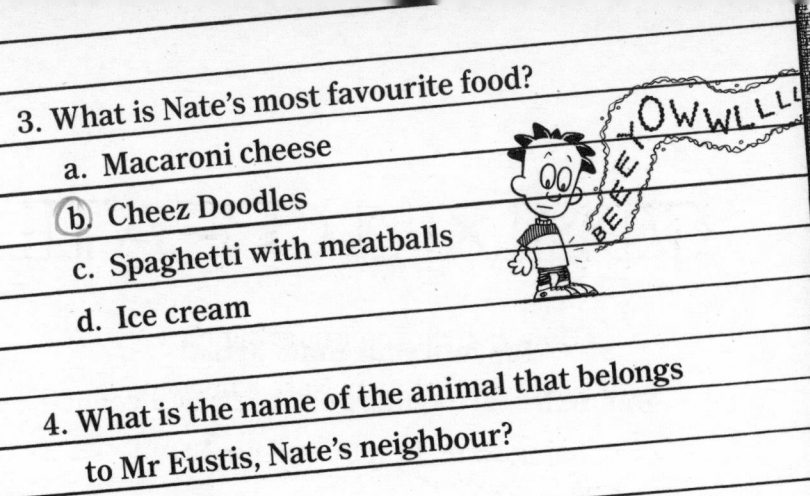

a. Macaroni cheese

b. Cheez Doodles

c. Spaghetti with meatballs

d. Ice cream

4. What is the name of the animal that belongs
to Mr Eustis, Nate's neighbour?

a. Pickles

b. Kuddles

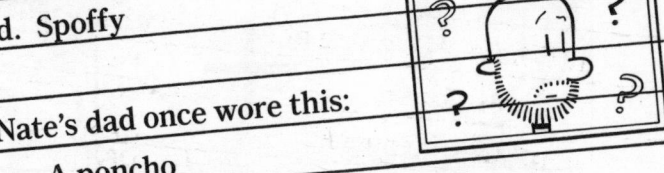

c. Spitsy

d. Spoffy

5. Nate's dad once wore this:

a. A poncho

b. Figure skates

c. Glasses

d. A Batman Halloween costume

COMIX U CREATE

Tap into your inner artist!
You're the cartooning genius. Draw a comic
using Nate, Randy, and pie NOW!

YOUR TITLE HERE

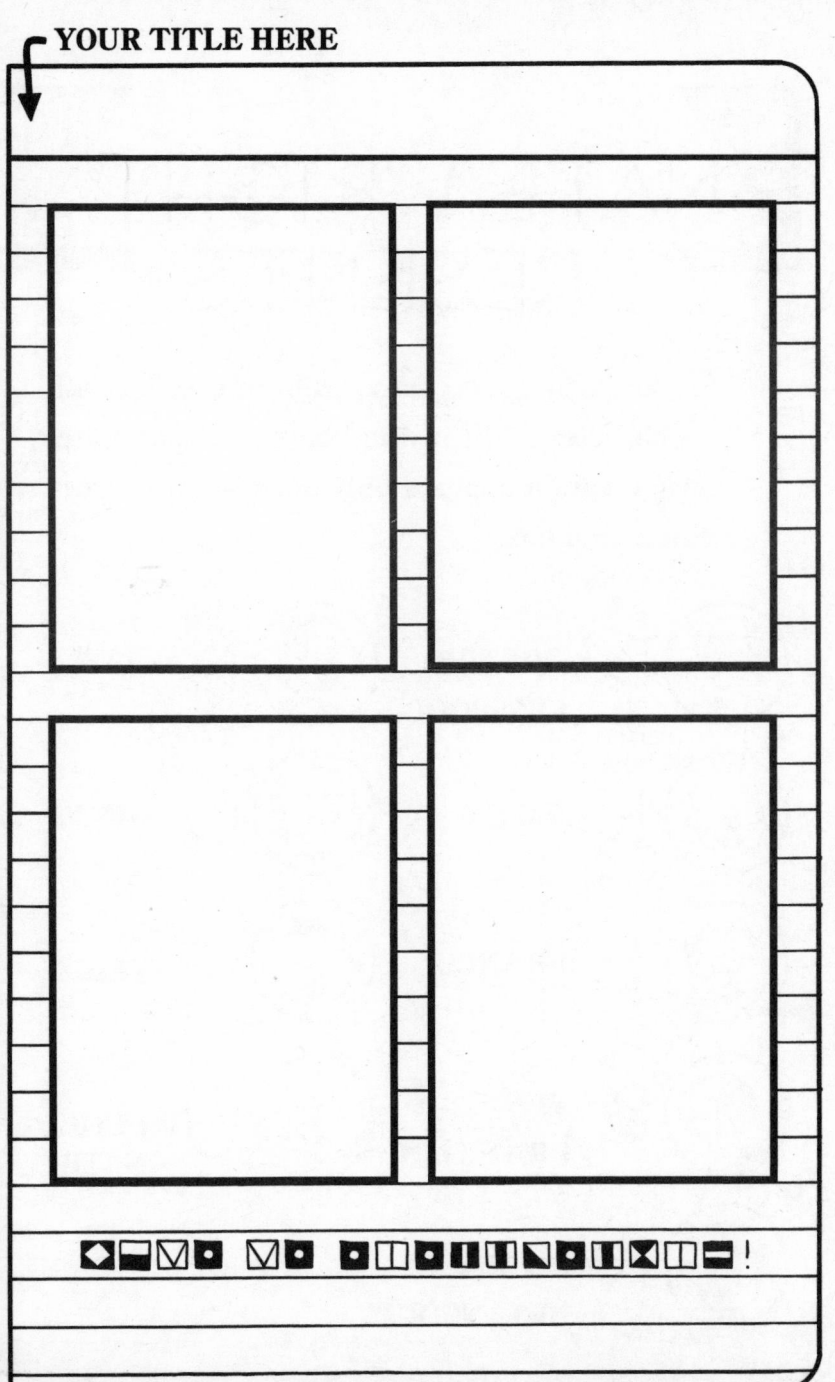

NATE WRIGHT PRESENTS

Nate loves to draw comix. Help him collect all his characters! Fill in the blanks so each Nate comix creation appears only once in every row, column, and box.

 **D** = DOCTOR CESSPOOL

 **N** = NATE

 **E** = ELLEN

 **G** = GINA

 **F** = FRANCIS

 **T** = TEDDY

 **B** = BEN FRANKLIN

 **U** = ULTRA-NATE

 **R** = RANDY BETANCOURT

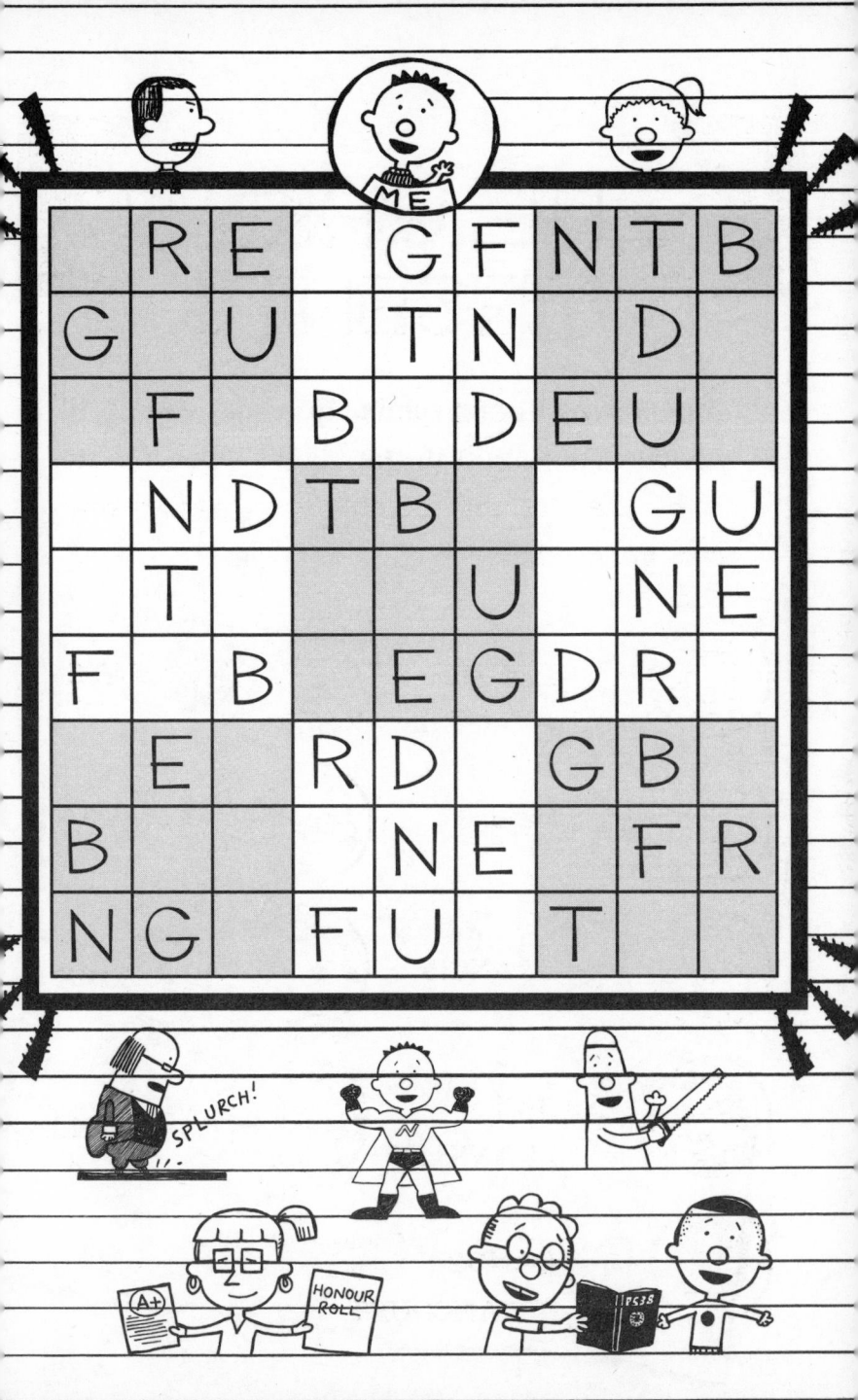

THE JOKE'S ON YOU!

Wanna laugh like crazy? Teddy's code (page 58) is the key to unlocking the hilarity!

Q: $\overline{\rm D}\ \overline{\rm S}\ \overline{\rm Z}\ \overline{\rm G}\ \ \overline{\rm W}\ \overline{\rm L}$

$\overline{\rm N}\ \overline{\rm L}\ \overline{\rm M}\ \overline{\rm H}\ \overline{\rm G}\ \overline{\rm V}\ \overline{\rm I}\ \overline{\rm H}\ \ \overline{\rm I}\ \overline{\rm V}\ \overline{\rm Z}\ \overline{\rm W}$

$\overline{\rm V}\ \overline{\rm E}\ \overline{\rm V}\ \overline{\rm I}\ \overline{\rm B}\ \ \overline{\rm W}\ \overline{\rm Z}\ \overline{\rm B}$?

HEH HEH!

A: $\overline{\rm G}\ \overline{\rm S}\ \overline{\rm V}\ \overline{\rm I}\ \overline{\rm I}$

$\overline{\rm S}\ \overline{\rm L}\ \overline{\rm I}\ \overline{\rm I}\ \overline{\rm L}\ \overline{\rm I}\ \overline{\rm H}\ \overline{\rm X}\ \overline{\rm L}\ \overline{\rm K}\ \overline{\rm V}$!

Q:
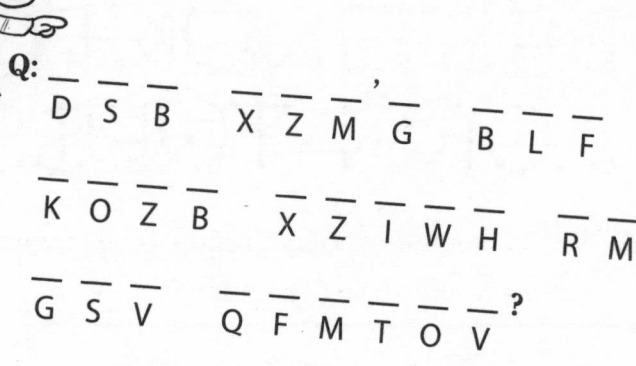

_ _ _   _ _ _ _ , _ _ _
D S B   X Z M G   B L F

_ _ _ _   _ _ _ _ _   _ _
K O Z B   X Z I W H   R M

_ _ _   _ _ _ _ _ _ ?
G S V   Q F M T O V

A:
_ _ _ _ _ _ _   _ _ _ _ _
Y V X Z F H V   G S V I V

_ _ _   _ _ _   _ _ _ _
Z I V   G L L   N Z M B

_ _ _ _ _ _ _ _ !
X S V V G Z S H

HONK!
HONK
HONK!

DESTINED FOR GREATNESS

Help Nate with his list!

NATE COULD ACHIEVE GREATNESS IN…

1. Football
2. Music
3. Cartooning
4. Table football
5.
6.
7.
8.
9.
10.

DESTINED FOR

GREATNESS!

HOW WILL YOU...

...SURPASS ALL OTHERS?

1. I'm in a rock band.
2. I will become a pilot.
3. I will swim with dolphins.
4.
5.
6.
7.
8.
9.
10.
11.
12.
13.
14.
15.

BATTER UP!

Take your team to victory! Draw lines from List A to List B to create the ultimate team names.

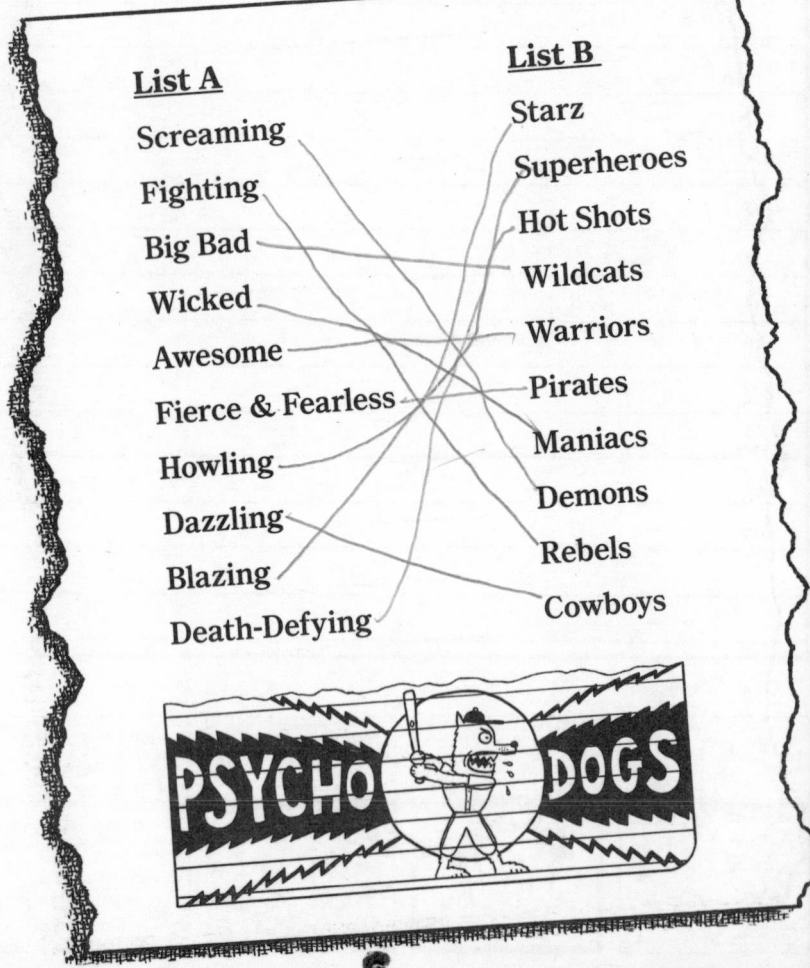

List A

Screaming

Fighting

Big Bad

Wicked

Awesome

Fierce & Fearless

Howling

Dazzling

Blazing

Death-Defying

List B

Starz

Superheroes

Hot Shots

Wildcats

Warriors

Pirates

Maniacs

Demons

Rebels

Cowboys

PSYCHO DOGS

WRITE YOUR ULTIMATE
TEAM NAMES HERE:

_____

_____

_____

_____

_____

_____

_____

_____

_____

_____

WHERE'S PICASSO?

Are you destined to be a talented artist like Picasso? Pick up that pencil! Draw your self-portrait.

 # BIG BEN

Nate's a serious Ben Franklin fan, because Ben was an inventor AND a cartoonist, just like Nate! See how inventive you can be. Using the letters in Ben's name, try coming up with 25 other words!

BEN FRANKLIN

1.	16.
2.	17.
3.	18.
4.	19.
5.	20.
6.	21.
7.	22.
8.	23.
9.	24.
10.	25.
11.	
12.	
13.	
14.	
15.	

CELEBRITY FOR A DAY

Nate knows he's going to hit it big some day! What if YOU became a star and everyone knew YOUR name? Do you aim for fame?

CIRCLE YOUR TOP 5
CELEBRITY PROFESSIONS

EL CAPITÁN

Hollywood actor/actress

Genius scientist

Pro athlete

Broadway dancer

Doctor

President

Musician/rock star

Famous artist

Astronaut

Author

Animal trainer

Deep sea diver

Inventor

Race car driver

Video game creator

NATE'S BABY BOOK

Check out Nate's baby picture! He wasn't the cutest baby on the planet – look at that spiky hair!

WHAT ARE YOUR BABY FACTS?
(How would you know? You were only a baby! Ask your parents!)

PLACE YOU WERE BORN:

Dundee

EYE COLOUR:

Blue

YOUR FIRST WORD:

Mama

AGE WHEN YOU FIRST CRAWLED:

8 months

FAVOURITE FOOD:

Banana Pudding

FAVOURITE TOY:

Pooh Bear

FUNNIEST HABIT:
(Did you suck your thumb?
Or talk in gibberish?)

getting excited

Me and Ellen

PERFECT
PARTNERS

Who will be Nate's partner for the school project?

DOODLE TIME!

Is your science teacher making you fall asleep?

Is your dad driving you crazy?

Then you know what time it is!

PET PARADISE

Meet Spitsy, the dog who lives next door to Nate! He's a little bit crazy. He wears a collar that makes him look like a walking satellite dish and he is scared of the mailman. See if you can find all 20 kinds of pet below in the animal scramble on the next page!

PARAKEET

FERRET

TURTLE

GOLDFIS

PARR T

HORSE

MOUSE

LIZARD

CANARY

IGUANA

BBIT

KITTEN

GUINEA PIG

SALAMANDER

SNAKE

HAMSTER

DOG

PIG

GERBIL

PONY

WURF!

G N O T G B K C T S W S L W H
Y Y T K H J H T A U N O T L S
F E R R E T Y L E A R U U R I
P Q J G M L A C K E B T E E F
A C Z O D M Y E U Y K T L L D
R G I P A E N I U G S A I E L
R C T N T T J M D M G Z R X O
O S D E I H M H A S A Z O A G
T E A U B O O H Y R A N A C P
R N Y N B A U R D G E R B I L
K Z T D A F S D S T X F G V X
Y G K M R U E O T E F T V O I
X I K D I Z G I A U D L D F D
Q S H E T W K I U A H B R Z T
Y N O P W X M X S V U A O X X

Z...

DID YOU KNOW?

Decode these facts using Francis's code.
See page 39 for code.

$\overline{6}\ \overline{1}\ \overline{8}$ $\overline{18}\ \overline{20}\ \overline{25}$ $\overline{11}\ \overline{26}\ \overline{8}\ \overline{13}\ \overline{21}$

$\overline{14}\ \overline{20}\ \overline{25}\ \overline{3}\ \overline{8}$ $\overline{20}\ \overline{24}$ $\overline{6}\ \overline{1}\ \overline{8}$

$\overline{23}\ \overline{13}\ \overline{14}\ \overline{3}\ \overline{8}\ \overline{24}\ \overline{6}$

$\overline{18}\ \overline{11}\ \overline{10}\ \overline{21}\ \overline{6}\ \overline{13}\ \overline{20}\ \overline{21}$ $\overline{14}\ \overline{13}\ \overline{21}\ \overline{3}\ \overline{8}$

$\overline{20}\ \overline{21}$ $\overline{6}\ \overline{1}\ \overline{8}$ $\overline{22}\ \overline{11}\ \overline{14}\ \overline{23}\ \overline{25}$,

$\overline{13}\ \overline{21}\ \overline{25}$ $\overline{20}\ \overline{6}$ $\overline{20}\ \overline{24}$

$\overline{10}\ \overline{21}\ \overline{25}\ \overline{8}\ \overline{14}\ \overline{22}\ \overline{13}\ \overline{6}\ \overline{8}\ \overline{14}$.

$\overline{6}$ $\overline{1}$ $\overline{8}$ $\overline{14}$ $\overline{8}$ $\overline{13}$ $\overline{14}$ $\overline{8}$ $\overline{13}$ $\overline{7}$ $\overline{11}$ $\overline{10}$ $\overline{6}$

$\overline{11}$ $\overline{21}$ $\overline{8}$ $\overline{1}$ $\overline{10}$ $\overline{21}$ $\overline{25}$ $\overline{14}$ $\overline{8}$ $\overline{25}$

$\overline{6}$ $\overline{14}$ $\overline{20}$ $\overline{23}$ $\overline{23}$ $\overline{20}$ $\overline{11}$ $\overline{21}$

$\overline{26}$ $\overline{8}$ $\overline{23}$ $\overline{23}$ $\overline{24}$ $\overline{20}$ $\overline{21}$ $\overline{6}$ $\overline{1}$ $\overline{8}$

$\overline{1}$ $\overline{10}$ $\overline{18}$ $\overline{13}$ $\overline{21}$ $\overline{7}$ $\overline{11}$ $\overline{25}$ $\overline{9}$.

REALLY? WHAT A **BRILLIANT** OBSERVATION, FRANCIS! I DIDN'T **KNOW** THAT!

CAN I SEE?

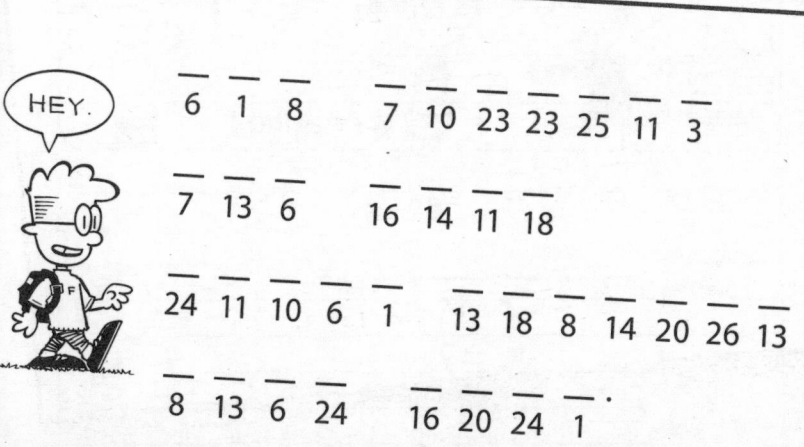

HEY.

$\overline{6}$ $\overline{1}$ $\overline{8}$ $\overline{7}$ $\overline{10}$ $\overline{23}$ $\overline{23}$ $\overline{25}$ $\overline{11}$ $\overline{3}$

$\overline{7}$ $\overline{13}$ $\overline{6}$ $\overline{16}$ $\overline{14}$ $\overline{11}$ $\overline{18}$

$\overline{24}$ $\overline{11}$ $\overline{10}$ $\overline{6}$ $\overline{1}$ $\overline{13}$ $\overline{18}$ $\overline{8}$ $\overline{14}$ $\overline{20}$ $\overline{26}$ $\overline{13}$

$\overline{8}$ $\overline{13}$ $\overline{6}$ $\overline{24}$ $\overline{16}$ $\overline{20}$ $\overline{24}$ $\overline{1}$.

HELP!
WHAT ARE THEY
SAYING?

You decide. Fill in the speech bubbles.

RAPPIN' AND RHYMIN'

Write a sentence that rhymes
with each underlined word.
You are a rapper!

YOU'VE HAD YOUR <u>FUN</u>,

_____ ,

YOU HEAR THEM <u>SAY</u>,

_____ .

NOW WE <u>FLY</u>,

_____ ,

AND THEN WE <u>MEET</u>,

_____ .

THE TIME IS <u>RIGHT</u>,

_____ ,

OH YES YOU <u>SEE</u>,

_____ .

WHO'S IN LOVE?

Nate likes Jenny. Jenny likes Artur. Nate hates Gina, but as Teddy says, "It's a fine line between hate and love." Nate needs help! Fill in the blanks so each person appears only once in every row, column and box.

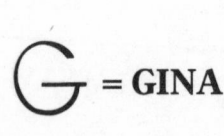 = GINA

 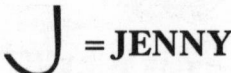 = NATE

= JENNY

 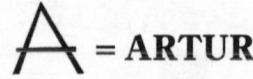 = ARTUR

HOW TO DRAW ME

**Follow Nate's step-by-step instructions
and bring him to life!**

HINT: SKETCH LIGHTLY AT FIRST, THEN MAKE LINES **BOLDER** TO FINISH YOUR DRAWING!

START WITH AN OVAL. SEE HOW IT'S WIDER AT THE TOP?

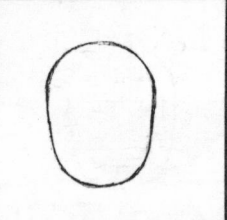

MAKE A SMALLER OVAL. THERE'S MY NOSE!

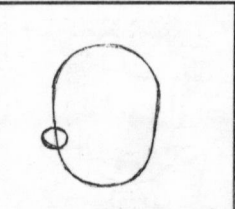

A LOOP (LIKE A BACKWARD "C") IS MY EAR.

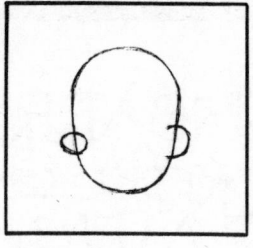

I HAVE SEVEN TUFTS OF HAIR. FOLLOW THE ARROWS!

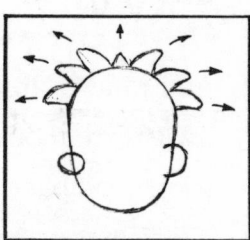

MY EYES ARE EASY TO DRAW. THEY'RE TWO STRAIGHT LINES!

NOW ADD MY MOUTH SO I CAN SAY SOMETHING!

COLOUR IN MY HAIR, ADD A NECK AND SHOULDERS, AND YOU'RE DONE!

MOST EMBARRASSING MOMENTS EVER

Do you ever wish you could run and hide? Nate's no stranger to awkward moments – he's the king of embarrassing situations. The worst was when he accidentally spilled egg salad on his crush Jenny's head!

GIVE EACH A MARK FROM 1 TO 10. 10 IS THE MOST EMBARRASSING!

9	Being caught picking your nose
8	Having to wear the ugly snowman sweater from Aunt Gladys to school
2	Slipping in the hall after the janitor waxed the floors
1	Throwing up on the roller coaster
1	When you show up wearing the same shirt as your lab partner
8	When your mum kisses you big time while dropping you off at school

9	Looking cross-eyed in your school pictures
9	The cat pees on your feet
1	When you're picked second-to-last in gym class
5	You're all ready to perform for the talent show and your voice gets all scratchy
10	Your hair is sticking straight up all day and you have no idea
10	Laughing so hard that snot comes out of your nose
9	You spill orange juice on your shirt at lunch and it looks like puke
10	You have to dance with your teachers at your school dance

MUSICAL MADNESS

Nate is the rockin' drummer in his band, Enslave the Mollusk! Now it's your turn. Take the stage and find all the instruments in this hidden word puzzle!

FLUTE

TROMBONE

TRUMPET

GUITAR

CYMBALS

TRIANGLE

SAXOPHONE

PIANO

VIOLIN

TUBA

BASS

VIOLA

DRUMS

FRENCH HORN

HARP

CLARINET

PICCOLO

TAMBOURINE

M	E	N	P	U	A	T	P	L	O	R	A
I	L	U	R	S	O	N	T	S	A	T	R
O	T	R	U	M	P	E	T	T	N	U	R
U	G	E	L	G	N	A	I	R	T	B	E
O	V	E	N	I	R	U	O	B	M	A	T
L	T	X	R	O	G	H	N	A	O	C	U
O	H	A	R	P	H	I	B	S	N	Y	L
C	L	O	L	C	L	P	A	S	U	M	F
C	V	E	N	O	B	M	O	R	T	B	Y
I	Y	E	I	A	I	E	L	X	A	A	C
P	R	V	A	M	I	V	G	E	A	L	T
F	D	R	U	M	S	P	T	S	S	S	B

WILD WORLD RECORDS

Nate knows he's got the right stuff to stand out. He's ready to surpass all others and set a world record! For longest fingernails? No! Speed eating? Maybe! He does LOVE Cheez Doodles!

CHECK OUT THESE SUPER WEIRD WORLD RECORDS:

Longest eyebrows
Largest feet
Longest nose
Tallest man
Highest hair
Biggest cookie
Fastest talker
Most T-shirts worn at once
Most worms swallowed
Most tennis balls held in one hand
Most consecutive pogo stick jumps
Longest nonstop TV watching

WHAT WOULD <u>YOU</u> SET A RECORD IN?

1.
2.
3.
4.
5. Biggest smile
6.
7.
8.
9. Loudest burp
10.
11.
12.
13. Most chocolate eaten
14.
15.

SUPER SCRIBBLE GAME

How fast can you play the scribble game?

Don't forget to write a caption for it:

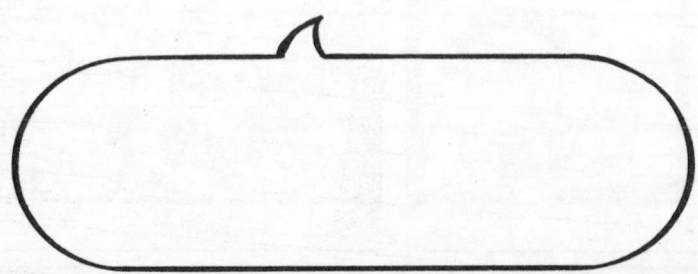

SCHOOL RULES

Nate cruises the school halls with confidence. But where does he always end up? DETENTION!

WHAT ARE YOUR ALL-TIME FAVOURITE SCHOOL SUBJECTS?

1.

2.

3.

4.

5.

Thank you and have a great day!

Did you hear the bell? School's in session. See if you can solve the puzzle and figure out all of Nate's daily subjects.

CLUES

ACROSS

3. Where you might make a birdhouse or a pencil box. (8)

4. Paying attention in this subject will help you solve this puzzle! (8)

8. Here "hola" means "hello." (7)

10. Nate's favourite class. (3)

11. You might practise these lines: "Romeo, O Romeo, wherefore art thou Romeo?" (5)

14. In this class, you might be allowed to go on www.bignatebooks.com! (8)

DOWN

1. How many continents are there? (6,7)

2. After lunch, you have _____ . (6)

5. Where you create a poetry portfolio. (7)

6. Let's pick teams. (3)

7. Name the basic food groups. (6)

9. Today we're going to dissect a frog. (7)

12. If x is 2 and y is 3, x + y = ? (5)

13. Tater tots and mystery meat. (5)

15. Who wants to play the triangle? (5)

HINT!

Nate's school subjects might have different names to yours.
Here are some clues:

GYM HEALTH RECESS SOCIAL STUDIES WOODSHOP

WHOA!
WHAT'S HAPPENING?

Fill in the speech bubbles

and create your own crazy comix!

ROCK AND ROLLIN'

It's time to rock out, Nate style! Fill in words below to create your own band names.

1. FUNKY _____ _____

_____ TIME

2. _____ _____

_____ DIAMOND _____

3. _____ DIAMOND _____

4. WILD _____ _____

_____ BLUE _____

5. _____ BLUE _____

_____ FORTUNE

6. _____ _____ FORTUNE

7. LAUGHING _____ _____

_____ SECRET _____

8. _____ SECRET _____

_____ MACHINE

9. _____ _____ MACHINE

10. GALAXY _____

FABULOUS FUN-O-METER

Use Nate's Fun-o-Meter and rank each activity!

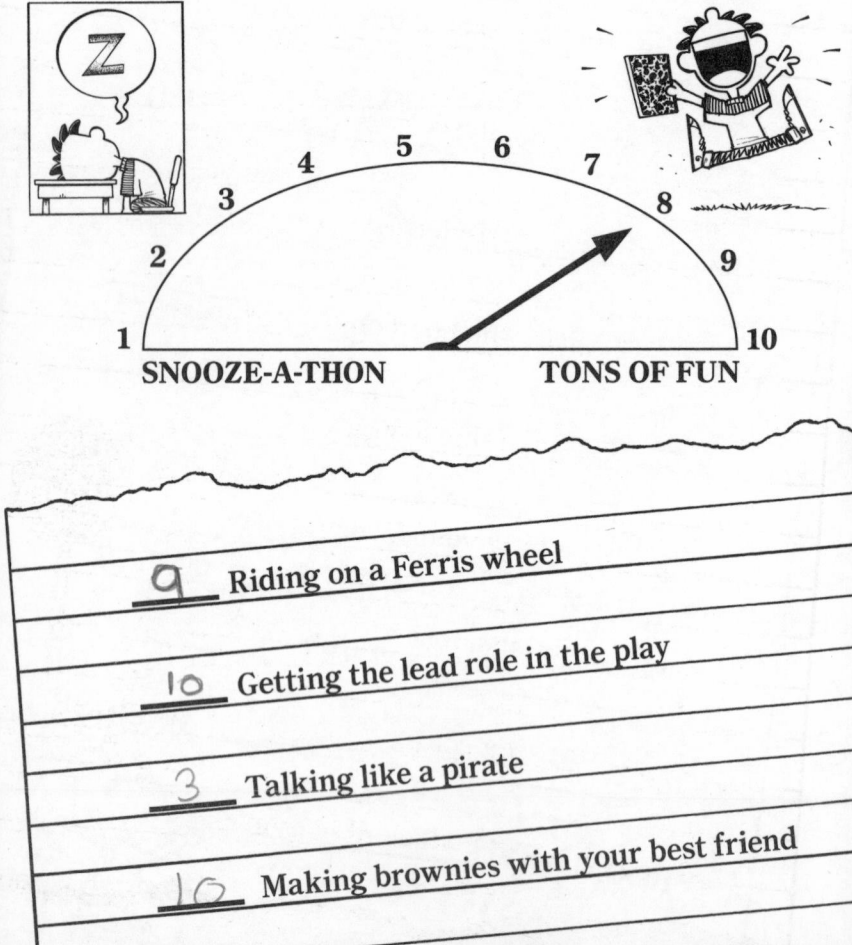

SNOOZE-A-THON   **TONS OF FUN**

_9_ Riding on a Ferris wheel

_10_ Getting the lead role in the play

_3_ Talking like a pirate

_10_ Making brownies with your best friend

2 Building a sandcastle

5 Watching the sun set

8 Trick-or-treating at Halloween

6 Riding the school bus

7 Eating candyfloss

4 Going to the dentist

8 Cruisin' the hood on your skateboard

3 Playing table football

NO
FUN
ALLOWED

1 Watching your favorite team

9 Building a fort

9 Drawing comix

10 Playing dodgeball in gym class

EPISODE 17: One day in the OPERATING ROOM...

EXTRA CREDIT

MRS GODFREY, DO YOU EVER TAKE A DAY OFF? YOU KNOW, JUST FOR A LITTLE BREAK?

NO.

IF I TOOK A DAY OFF JUST BECAUSE I FELT LIKE IT, WHO WOULD TEACH YOU STUDENTS?

I DON'T WANT YOU KIDS LEARNING THIS STUFF ON THE STREET.

THEY TEACH ABOUT THE WEBSTER-ASHBURTON TREATY ON THE STREET?

SOUNDS LIKE A FUN NEIGHBOURHOOD.

3/19

© 2009 by NEA, Inc.

SUPER SPOFF

What's a SPOFF? The coolest thing ever!

Nate's dying to win the SPOFF championship and take home the ultimate prize – the Spoffy! Help him find all the hidden words so he can surpass all others!

G	O	G	L	S	Z	L	U	E	C	A	O	F	L
R	E	M	A	L	L	H	R	Y	L	L	D	T
D	E	H	R	T	A	A	F	U	E	O	P	K	L
E	R	O	H	D	E	B	A	R	O	L	E	S	A
G	A	L	F	E	H	T	E	R	U	T	P	A	C
M	U	R	R	H	N	O	H	G	P	U	H	F	T
O	Q	U	E	B	T	O	C	E	D	B	A	A	E
O	S	E	E	A	C	F	T	O	R	O	B	A	M
A	R	H	Z	K	T	G	O	N	R	B	D	E	D
H	U	A	E	A	G	A	C	E	I	E	A	U	D
G	O	Y	T	G	E	L	S	R	S	M	Y	L	T
E	F	N	A	C	E	F	P	R	E	F	D	R	L
D	U	E	G	R	E	V	O	R	D	E	R	A	H
Z	F	G	E	V	S	H	H	S	U	D	L	S	B

CAPTURE THE FLAG

BADMINTON

FOURSQUARE

TETHERBALL

RED ROVER

FREEZE TAG

HOPSCOTCH

HORSE

WHACK!

WHO DO YOU THINK YOU ARE?

SPOTLIGHT ON...

YOU

Nickname: **Rox Man**

Birthday: **1E DCO 4 Jni £**

Astrological sign: Pisces

Song you play over and over: **Nothing by Nobody**

Most amazing book you've ever read: Harry Potter **50000 Marks**

Coolest place you've travelled to: **hAir loved**

Best friend: **Plunger man** H, Robbn

Jay

Pet: None

Celebrity crush: None

Greatest movie you've ever seen: Harry Potter

Dream job: Author

Biggest talent: Writing books

Favorite time of year: Birthday

Your signature dance move: None

#1 for weekend fun: ?

Best place on Earth: Greece

Proudest moment:

Your hero:

NO LESSON PLAN!

Not every teacher is boring. Help Nate find the fun teachers at P.S. 38. Fill in the blanks so each appears only once in every row, column, and box.

R = **MR ROSA**

S = **MRS SHIPULSKI**

H = **MRS HICKSON**

C = **COACH CALHOUN**

OUT-OF-CONTROL LOCKER

**Nate's locker is overflowing with cool stuff –
no joke! What are your must-haves for your locker?**

TOP 25 MUST-HAVES:

1. *a toilet of the gold Pool!)*
2. Smelly socks *of poop*
3.
4. Poster of *POOPPY!!!!*
   (Fill in your favourite celebrity!)
5. *lax*
6. *earwax*

7.

8.

9.

10. Cheez Doodles **FAIL**~~ ~~ ~ ~

11.

12.

13.

14.

15. Gym clothes

16.

17.

18.

19.

20.

21.

22.

23.

24.

25.

KLIK!

LIFE IS CRAZY

Life can be kind of crazy sometimes... you never know what might happen! You decide the story behind each scene.

THIS DOESN'T LOOK GOOD!

YIKES!

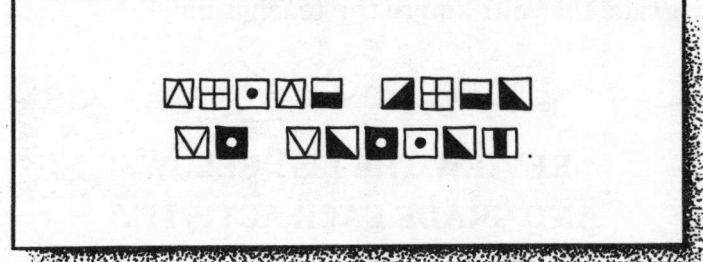

WHAT'S GOING ON?

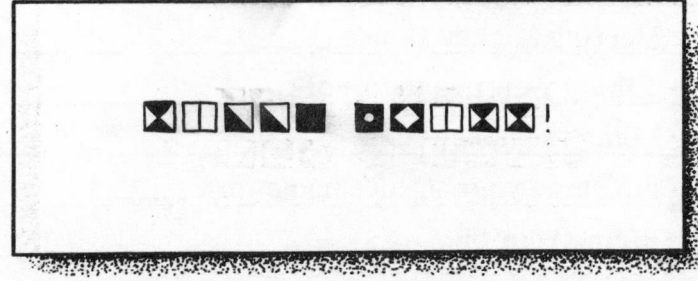

MAKING THE GRADE

Are you an A student all the way? What makes the grade for you? You're the teacher now!

**REVIEW THE LIST BELOW
AND GRADE EACH ACTIVITY:
A, B, C, D, OR… (UH-OH) F!**

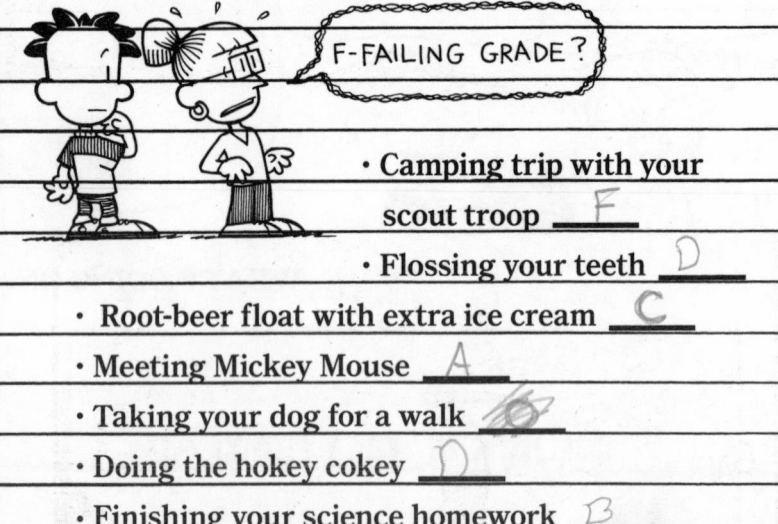

F-FAILING GRADE?

- Camping trip with your scout troop __F__
- Flossing your teeth __D__
- Root-beer float with extra ice cream __C__
- Meeting Mickey Mouse __A__
- Taking your dog for a walk __B__
- Doing the hokey cokey __D__
- Finishing your science homework __B__
- Riding your bike __A__

- **Climbing the rope in gym class** _A_
- **Burping the alphabet** _C_
- **Skipping down the street** _F_
- **Taking out the garbage** _F_
- **Flying down a water slide** _A_
- **Eating gummy worms** _A_
- **Making up a dance routine** _F_
- **Going to your grandma's house** _B_
- **Washing the dishes** _F_
- **Giving your cousin a piggyback ride** _C_
- **Running for class president** _B_
- **Decorating your room** _F_

COMIX CRUSH

You are a cartoonist extraordinaire! Make the
funniest comic about Nate, Spitsy, and Jenny!

YOUR TITLE HERE

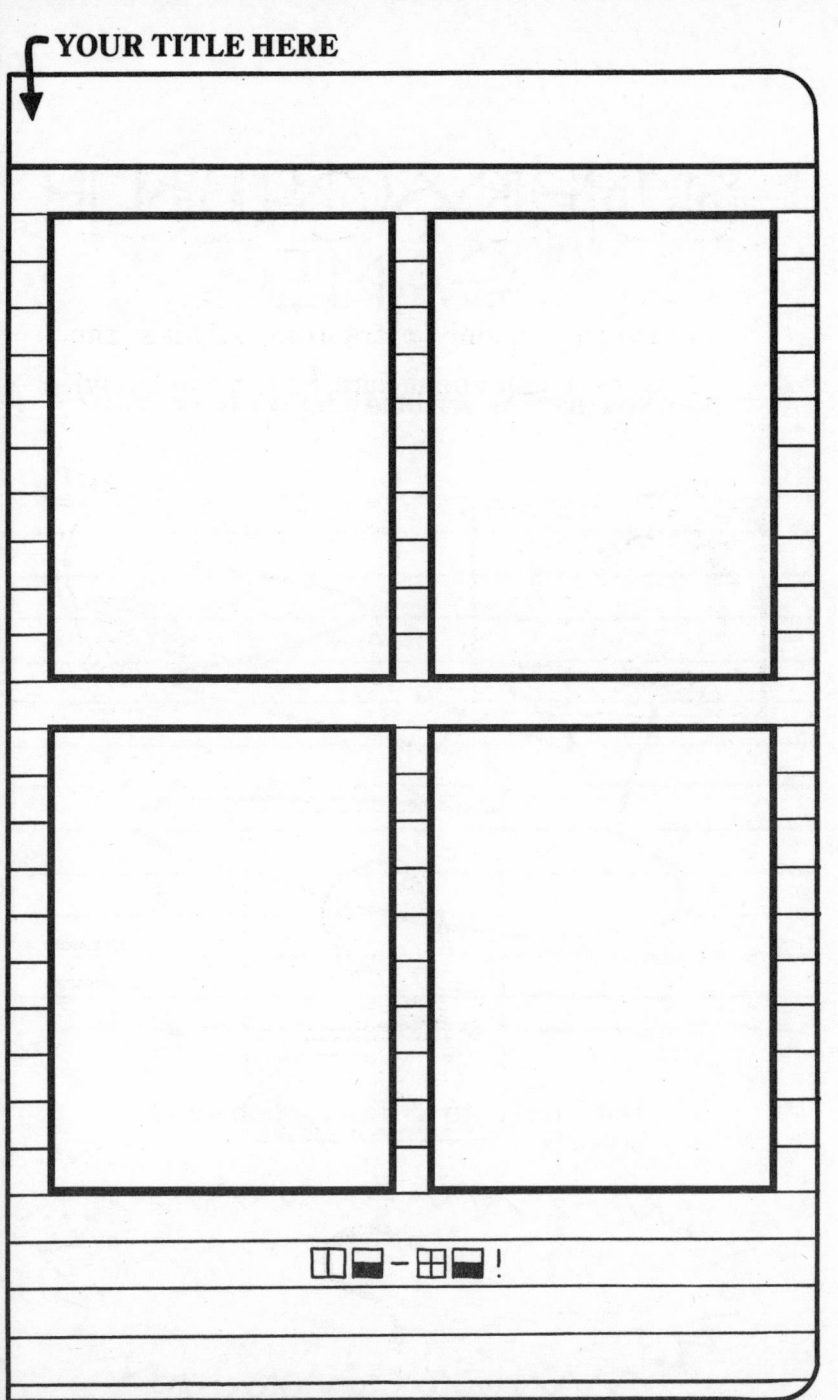

SUPER SCRIBBLE GAME

Can you play the scribble game in 10 seconds?

Don't forget to write a caption for it:

SHOWDOWN!

Mrs Godfrey would rather be eating lemon squares.

CHEER CLUB

Nate's no cheerleader, but he sure looks cute in his uniform! Just kidding. Still, Nate has TONS of spirit – he's his own biggest fan! Help cheer Nate on to greatness!

FINISH THE CHEERS.
RHYME WITH THE UNDERLINED WORD!

Our team's on top, our team's on <u>top</u>,
Once we start we can't be _stopped_

We're number one, we're not number <u>two</u>,
We're gonna beat the socks off _you_.

Our team won't take <u>defeat</u>,
Our team won't feel the _____,
Our team just can't be _beat_!

NOW MAKE UP YOUR OWN CHEERS!

Hey, hey, get out of our way,
'Cause today is the day we will _____ .

Everybody in the stands,
Clap your _____ .

Come on team, let's have some fun,
Come on team, we're number _____ !

We've got spirit, yes we do!
We've got spirit, how 'bout _____ ?

OUTBURSTS!

What's going on in each picture?
Fill in the speech bubbles!

WIDE WORLD OF NATE

Nate knows he's a big deal, and so is his name!
Using the letters in his name, see if you can make
at least 20 other words!

BIG NATE

1.
2.
3.
4.
5.
6.
7.
8.
9.
10.
11.
12.
13.
14.
15.
16.
17.
18.
19.
20.

NATE IQ TEST

What makes Nate tick? How much do you know about Nate, the notorious mischief-maker?

CIRCLE THE CORRECT ANSWER!

1. What's the name of Nate's comic strip?
   a. Max, the Mad Scientist
   b. Kooky Carl
   c. Daredevil Marvin
   d. Doctor Cesspool
   e. Magician Harry and Rex Rabbit

2. In which sport does Nate become a captain?
   a. Basketball
   b. Football
   c. Fleeceball
   d. Baseball
   e. Table football

THINK THINK THINK THINK THINK THIN THINK

3. What is Nate's next-door neighbour's name?

a. Mrs Shipulski

b. Mr Galvin

c. Mr Eustis

d. Mr Nichols

e. Mrs Czerwicki

4. Which is the one period where Nate hasn't gotten detention?

a. English

b. Art

c. Gym

d. Lunch

e. None of the above

** EXTRA CREDIT: Nate and Gina have to work together on a school project about…

a. Christopher Columbus

b. George Washington

c. Ben Franklin

d. Betsy Ross

e. Thomas Jefferson

** EXTRA EXTRA CREDIT:

‾‾ ‾‾ ‾‾ ‾‾   ‾‾ ‾‾ ‾‾'   ‾‾ ‾‾ ‾‾ ‾‾ ‾‾ ‾‾ !
 G S R H   L M V   T V M R F H

BEFORE I HAND IN THIS QUIZ, MRS GODFREY, I WANT TO SAY THAT I KNOW I DIDN'T DO WELL. AS YOU'LL SEE, I WASN'T FULLY PREPARED.

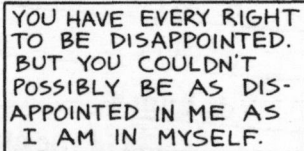

YOU HAVE EVERY RIGHT TO BE DISAPPOINTED. BUT YOU COULDN'T POSSIBLY BE AS DISAPPOINTED IN ME AS I AM IN MYSELF.

OH, YES I COULD.

SO MUCH FOR YOUR "PREEMPTIVE STRIKE" THEORY!

MUST BE NICE TO BE SO SURE OF YOURSELF ALL THE TIME.

MASTERMIND

Are you a whiz with words? Test your super skills!
Using the letters in "encyclopedia" below, see if you
can create 30 other words!

ENCYCLOPEDIA

1.	16.
2.	17.
3.	18.
4.	19.
5.	20.
6.	21.
7.	22.
8.	23.
9.	24.
10.	25.
11.	26.
12.	27.
13.	28.
14.	29.
15.	30.

LAUGH-A-MINUTE

What's so funny? Write speech bubbles and go for the BIGGEST laughs!

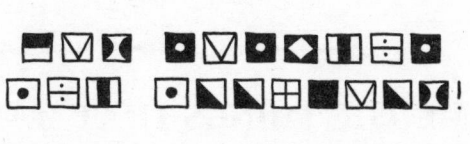

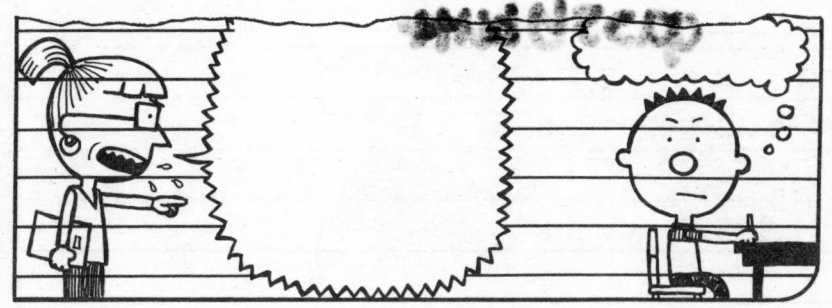

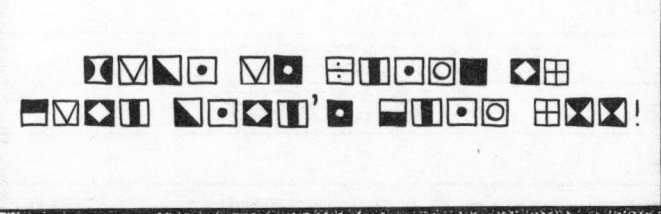

ONE OF A KIND

Nate's known for his super-spiky hair (check it out!) and his genius ideas... or at least he thinks so! What makes

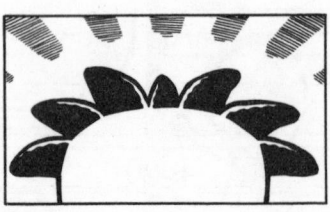

you unique? How do you stand out from the crowd?

NAME THE THINGS THAT MAKE YOU ONE OF A KIND:

1. ~~gassy butt~~
2.
3. Killer laugh
4.
5. Sassy smirk
6.
7.
8.
9.
10.
11.

12. Sweet football skills

13.

14.

15.

16. Funny faces

17.

18.

19.

20.

21. Colourful socks OF POO

22.

23.

24.

25.

ATHLETE OF THE YEAR

Nate loves sports. Well… most sports. Fill in the blanks so each sport appears only once in every row, column and box.

 **V** = **VOLLEYBALL**

 **Y** = **YOGA**

 **B** = **BASKETBALL**

 **H** = **HOCKEY**

 **T** = **TABLE FOOTBALL**

 **S** = **SOCCER**

 **D** = **DODGEBALL**

 **F** = **FLEECE-BALL**

 **R** = **RHYTHMIC GYMNASTICS**

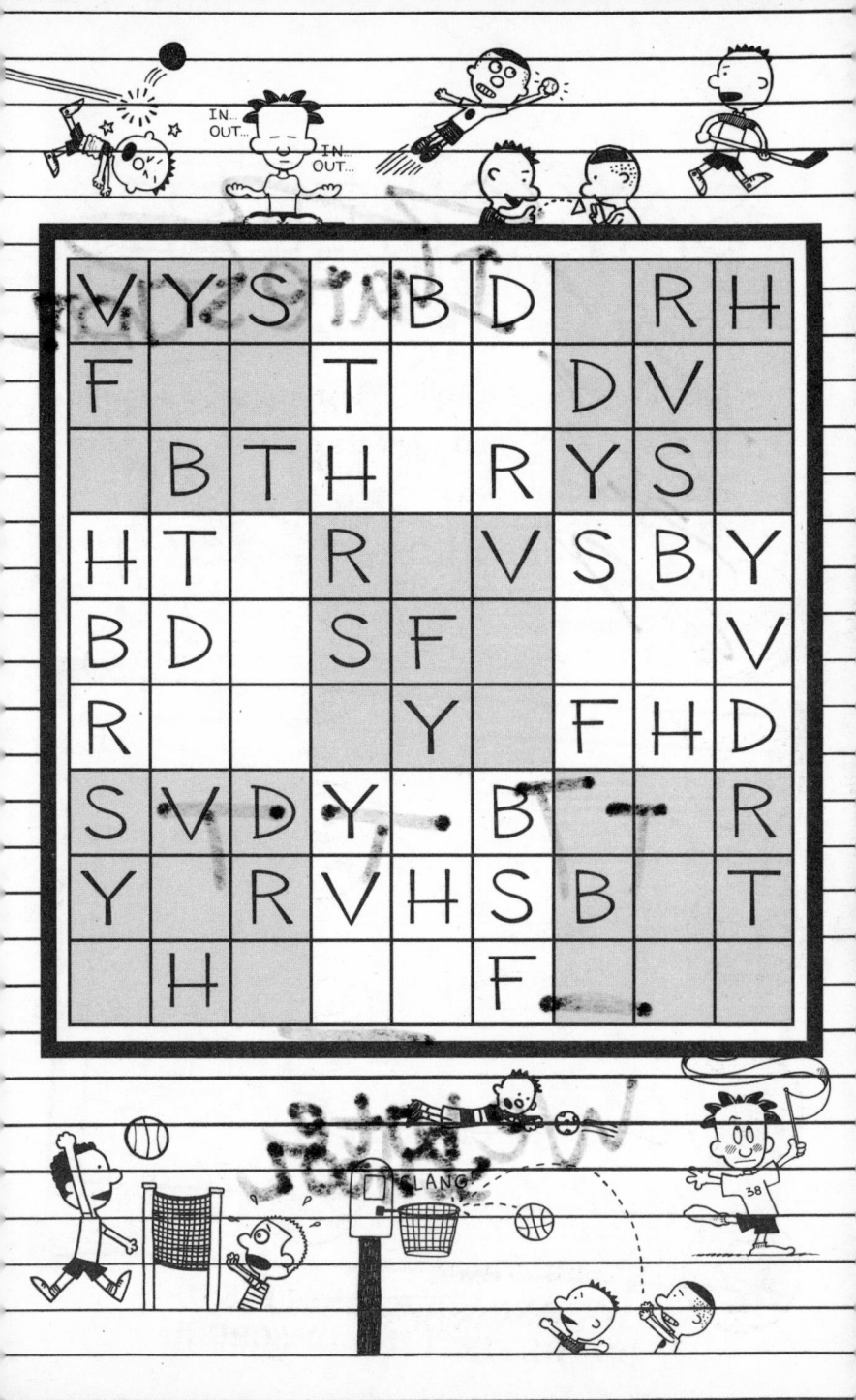

SAY ~~CHEESE!~~ I hate school

Smile BIG – it's time for your photo op! Create your own photo album by drawing in these major moments.

Me and Ellen

TT T T

‒ ‒

We ~~hate school~~

YOU AND YOUR BEST FRIEND ON THE FIRST DAY OF SCHOOL

YOUR BEST BIRTHDAY PARTY EVER

YOUR COOLEST HALLOWEEN COSTUME

SHOUT IT OUT!

What are these characters saying? Fill in the speech bubbles!

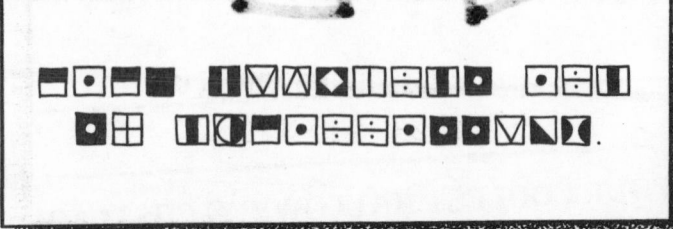

COMIX BY U!

You're the cartoonist now! Create a comic using
Mrs Godfrey, Nate, and a detention slip!

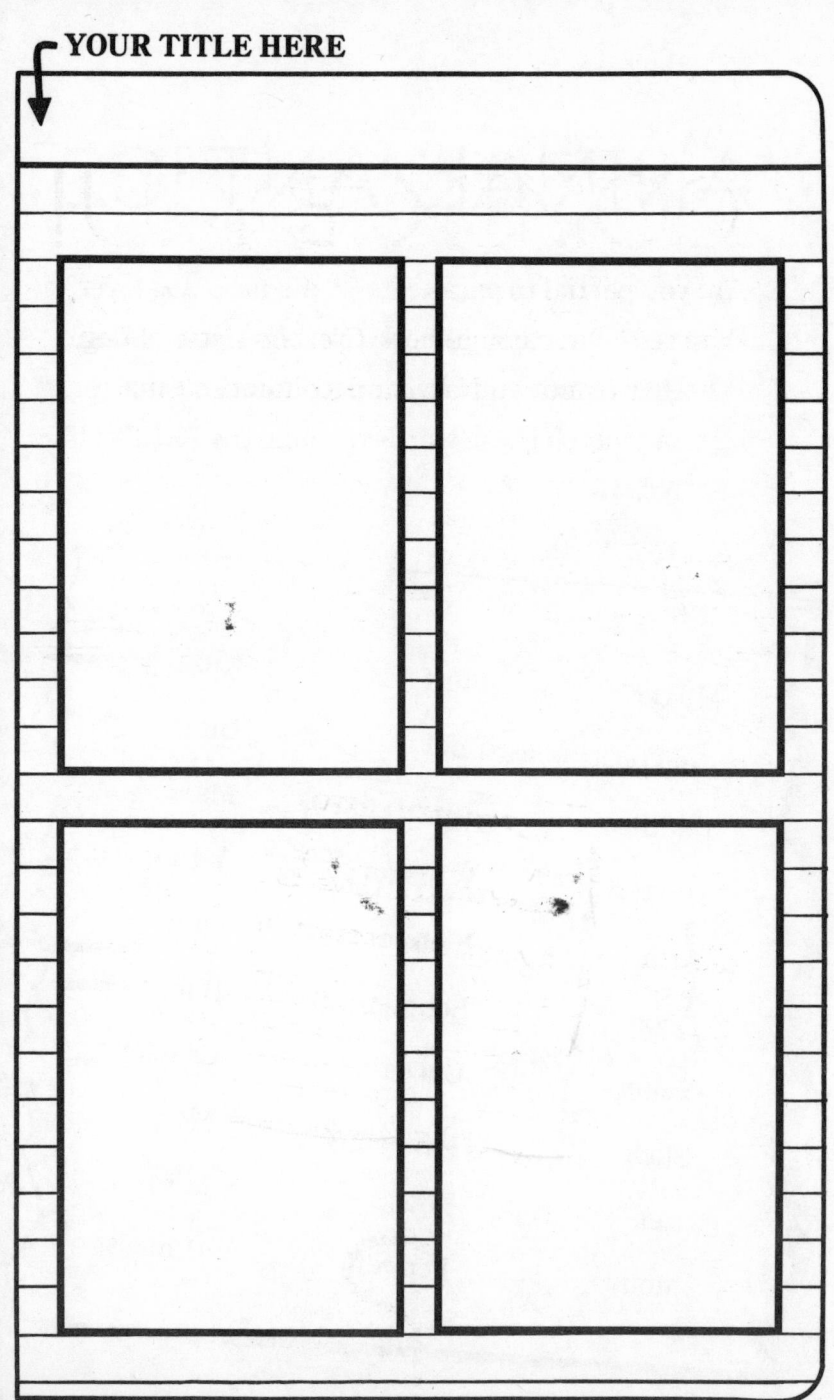

YOUR TITLE HERE

ANIMAL ANTICS

Are you partial to parakeets? A die-hard dog lover?
Or crazy for cats, like Nate's big sister, Ellen?
Whether or not you have a pet, it doesn't matter.
Mix and match these words to make the PERFECT
PET NAME!

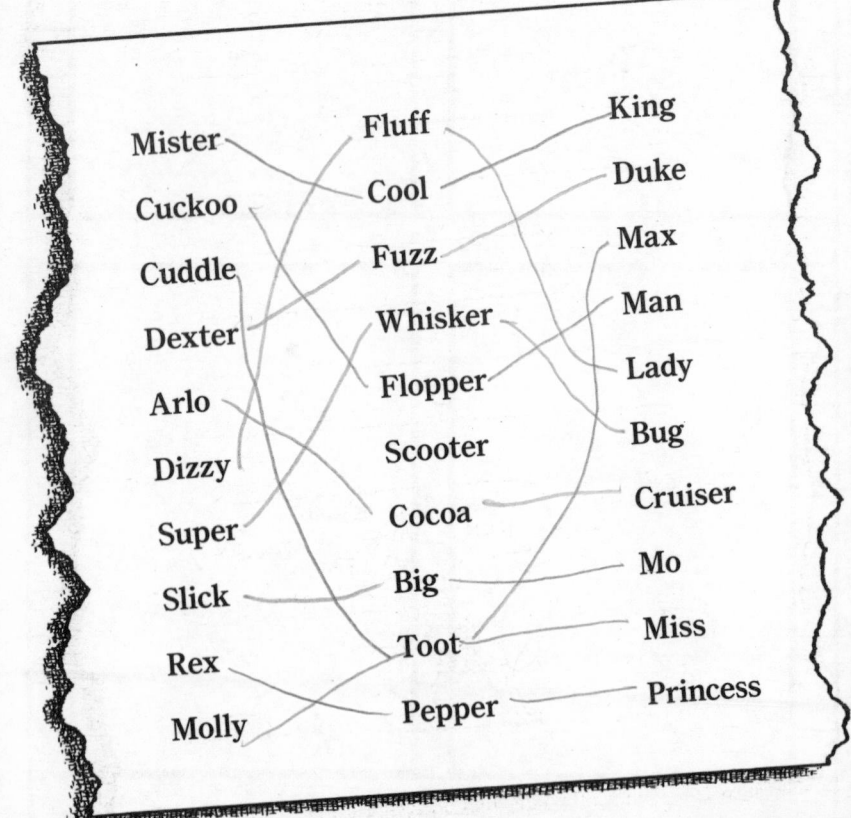

Mister Fluff King

Cuckoo Cool Duke

Cuddle Fuzz Max

Dexter Whisker Man

Arlo Flopper Lady

Dizzy Scooter Bug

Super Cocoa Cruiser

Slick Big Mo

Rex Toot Miss

Molly Pepper Princess

WRITE YOUR PERFECT
PET NAMES HERE:

_____

_____

_____

_____

_____

_____

_____

_____

_____

_____

_____

_____

BEST DAYS
EVER!

What makes you happier than ever? Describe your top 15 dream days!

BEST DAYS EVER

1.

2.

3. Winning the _____ tournament
(put in your favourite sport)

4.

5.

6.

7. Unlimited
Halloween candy!

8.

9.

10. When your crush talks to you for the first time EVER

11.

12.

13.

14.

15.

ANSWER KEY

NATE'S TOP SECRET CODE (p. 5)
Busted!
Oh, how I hate her!
Clueless as usual

INVENT-A-COMIX (p. 9)
Semaphore: Spike it, Ben!

CAST OF CHARACTERS (pp. 11–13)
My best friend
My worst enemy
Bossy older sister
My other best friend
Does not know how to work the DVD player
Annoying rival
My true love
Big bully
Drama queen
Ultimate dog nerd
Nate calls him Todd
Forces Nate to slow dance with her

POETRY SLAM: RHYME TIME
(pp. 24–25)
Semaphores:
You are a poet and you did not know it.
A Limerick to Mrs Godfrey
She is called by the name of Godzilla,
And yes, she's one scary gorilla,
Watch out or she'll eat you,
Her pop quizzes will beat you,
If you act just like Gina, you'll thrill her.

POP QUIZ! (p. 29)

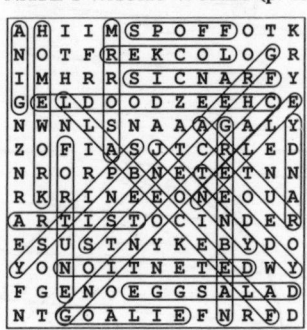

NATE'S WACKY WORLD (p. 19)

Maths—   Gym—   Social Studies—

Science—   English—   Art—

QUESTION OF THE DAY (p. 30)
None! That is what students are for!

COOL COMIX! (p. 33)
Semaphore: Now you are a cartooning genius,
just like Nate!

FRANCIS'S FANTASTIC SECRET ALPHABET (p. 39)
In *Big Nate on a Roll*, look out for Peter Pan, Timber Scouts,
and detention, of course.

BEST BUDS
(p. 35)

N	F	S	T
S	T	F	N
T	S	N	F
F	N	T	S

IN THE CAFETORIUM (p. 44)

	R						T		B		
S	P	I	N	A	C	H		U		R	
	C						N		U		
	E	G	G	S			A		S		
	C						F		S		
P	E	A				L	I	V	E	R	
	K		M				S		L		
C	E	L	E	R	Y		H		S		
			A						S		S
T	O	M	A	T	O				P		N
									R		A
			B	R	O	C	C	O	L	I	
									U		L
									T		
F	I	S	H	F	I	N	G	E	R	S	

DAD IS NOT A BLAST (p. 51)

1. True
2. False
3. True
4. False

CHEEZ DOODLE ALERT (p. 55)

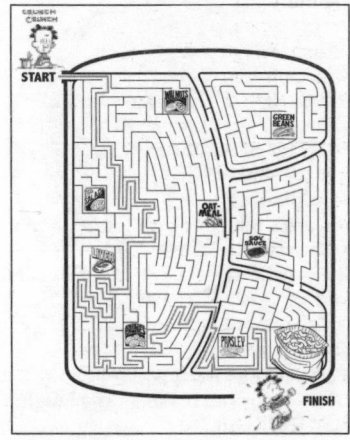

THE CHAMP (p. 46)

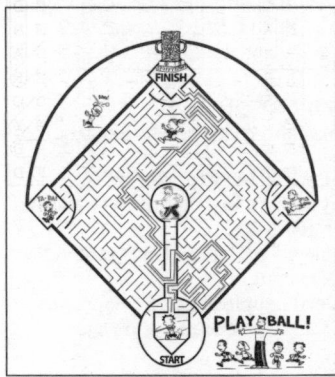

ANOTHER TEST! (pp. 56–57)

1.	False	7.	False
2.	True	8.	False
3.	False	9.	False
4.	False	10.	True
5.	True	11.	True
6.	True	12.	False

TEDDY'S TOP SECRET CODE (p. 59)

All MLB umpires must wear black underwear while on the job!
The tallest player in the NBA is currently Yao Ming.
He is seven feet, six inches.

IT'S CRAZY IN 3010! (p. 64)

Semaphore: The future is calling you!

DRAW-A-THON (p. 67)
Semaphore: Table football is one of Nate's best sports.

TEACHER TROUBLE (p. 69)

S	G	C	P
C	P	G	S
P	C	S	G
G	S	P	C

COSMIC COOKIES (p. 70)
You have a secret admirer.
You will live in the lap of luxury.
You will travel to the moon.

WEIRD BUT TRUE (p. 73)
The titan beetle can grow up to eight inches in length.

TRASHED! (p. 81)

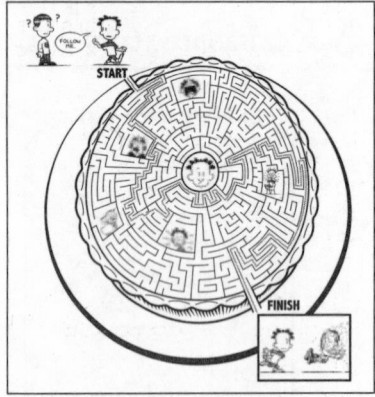

THE GANG'S ALL HERE! (p. 87)

S	D	G	A	N	T	F	J	E
F	T	J	E	S	G	N	A	D
N	A	E	F	J	D	S	T	G
A	J	F	T	G	E	D	N	S
T	E	S	N	D	J	A	G	F
D	G	N	S	A	F	T	E	J
E	S	T	G	F	A	J	D	N
G	N	D	J	T	S	E	F	A
J	F	A	D	E	N	G	S	T

COMIX BY U! (p. 89)
Semaphore: This smells like trouble!

GUESS WHAT? (pp. 96–97)
A python in Australia once swallowed four golf balls.
Monkeys in Thailand are trained to pick coconuts.
In Peru people ate chili peppers as long as six thousand years ago.

TOP JOKESTER (pp. 90–91)
Q: How can you make an egg laugh?
A: Tell it a yolk!
Q: What has two hands but can't clap?
A: A clock!

TRUE LIFE COMIX (p. 99)
Semaphore: One day this will be worth a lot of money!

ULTRA-NATE'S COMIX HEROES (p. 101)

E	O	A	E	M	R	A	R	E	W	Y	B	C	T	F
W	T	E	T	Y	P	O	O	N	S	E	A	H	F	K
O	D	A	H	N	E	K	U	D	A	M	R	A	M	X
L	E	E	S	U	P	E	R	M	A	N	R	R	L
V	E	N	J	F	I	E	O	Y	W	T	E	L	L	O
E	I	R	O	N	M	A	N	P	A	H	N	I	N	R
R	F	K	K	A	E	M	N	S	R	K	A	E	B	M
I	R	L	E	X	L	U	T	H	O	R	M	B	A	E
N	A	M	R	E	D	I	P	S	C	X	O	R	T	B
E	G	T	I	R	C	E	I	H	M	R	W	O	M	N
X	A	U	E	F	E	L	I	N	M	O	T	W	A	S
I	L	W	O	N	D	E	R	W	O	M	A	N	N	U
K	L	U	H	E	L	B	I	D	E	R	C	N	I	N
A	R	E	C	E	U	I	H	C	D	W	N	L	N	I
X	A	I	A	Y	A	A	O	E	P	M	H	L	A	L

EAT!.. EAT! EAT!

THE FORTU-NA-TOR (p. 106)

HONOUR ROLL, OR NOT? (p. 114)

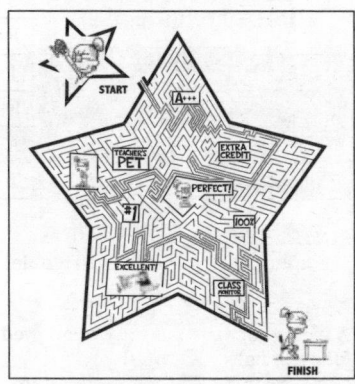

PERFECT PARTNERS (p. 138)

SAVED BY THE BELL (p. 109)

N	G	Y	A	T	E	I	R	H	G	S	I	C	L	O
N	N	R	L	J	T	I	O	N	E	C	G	N	L	T
U	I	E	Q	K	O	C	I	P	E	D	F	W	A	L
P	D	T	I	H	K	T	H	S	N	F	N	P	B	L
X	A	T	C	E	N	X	K	A	Q	R	D	V	K	E
L	E	O	Y	I	P	A	B	Q	E	A	O	I	C	B
L	L	P	A	E	T	I	M	P	N	K	M	D	I	S
A	R	P	T	I	V	M	A	C	M	R	P	E	K	I
B	E	U	N	A	T	P	I	N	U	J	J	O	R	R
E	E	G	U	E	L	N	H	P	O	V	K	G	E	F
S	H	S	L	O	G	S	G	N	I	T	C	A	A	N
A	C	L	O	G	N	O	P	G	N	I	P	M	D	I
R	A	H	A	E	T	A	R	A	K	W	W	E	I	A
B	C	L	L	A	B	T	E	K	S	A	B	S	N	B
S	T	R	N	B	O	B	A	Q	M	L	Z	A	G	C

TRIVIA TEST! (pp. 120–121)
1. (c) Mr Staples
2. (d) Gina
3. (b) Cheez Doodles
4. (c) Spitsy
5. (b) Figure skates

COMIX U CREATE (p. 123)
Semaphore: This is suspenseful!

NATE WRIGHT PRESENTS (p. 125)

D	R	E	U	G	F	N	T	B
G	B	U	E	T	N	R	D	F
T	F	N	B	R	D	E	U	G
E	N	D	T	B	R	F	G	U
R	T	G	D	F	U	B	N	E
F	U	B	N	E	G	D	R	T
U	E	F	R	D	T	G	B	N
B	D	T	G	N	E	U	F	R
N	G	R	F	U	B	T	E	D

THE JOKE'S ON YOU! (pp. 126–127)
Q: What do monsters read every day?
A: Their horrorscope!
Q: Why can't you play cards in the jungle?

PET PARADISE (p. 141)

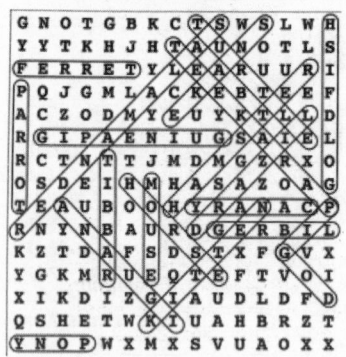

A: Because there are too many cheetahs!

DID YOU KNOW? (pp. 142–143)

The mid-ocean ridge is the largest mountain range in the world, and it is underwater.

There are about one hundred trillion cells in the human body.

The bulldog bat from South America eats fish.

WHO'S IN LOVE? (p. 147)

G	N	A	J
J	A	N	G
N	J	G	A
A	G	J	N

MUSICAL MADNESS (p. 153)

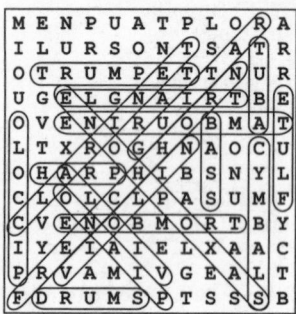

SCHOOL RULES (p. 159)

EXTRA CREDIT (p. 165)

Semaphore: Does Mrs Godfrey take her job too seriously? You decide!

SUPER SPOFF (p. 167)

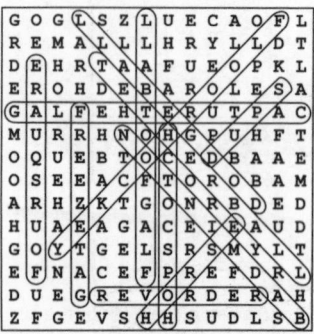

NO LESSON PLAN! (p. 171)

S	C	H	R
H	R	C	S
R	H	S	C
C	S	R	H

LIFE IS CRAZY (pp. 174–175)

Semaphores: Does Nate have a twin? Coach John is insane. Funny stuff!

COMIX CRUSH (p. 179)

Semaphore: Uh-oh!

SHOWDOWN! (p. 181)

OUTBURSTS! (pp. 184–185)
Semaphores: Goody Two-shoes
She looks mad!
Heads up!

NATE IQ TEST (pp. 188-190)
1.   (d) Doctor Cesspool
2.   (c) Fleeceball
3.   (c) Mr Eustis
4.   (e) None of the above
Extra Credit (c) Ben Franklin
Extra Extra Credit (Semaphore):
What test has only four questions?
(Teddy code): This one, genius!

MASTERMIND (p. 191)
Semaphore: Wow! You're a brainiac!

LAUGH-A-MINUTE (pp. 192–193)
Semaphores: Why is Nate smiling?
Big sisters are annoying!
Gina is ready to bite Nate's head off!

ATHLETE OF THE YEAR (p. 197)

V	Y	S	F	B	D	T	R	H
F	R	H	T	S	Y	D	V	B
D	B	T	H	V	R	Y	S	F
H	T	F	R	D	V	S	B	Y
B	D	Y	S	F	H	R	T	V
R	S	V	B	Y	T	F	H	D
S	V	D	Y	T	B	H	F	R
Y	F	R	V	H	S	B	D	T
T	H	B	D	R	F	V	Y	S

SHOUT IT OUT! (pp. 200–201)
Semaphores: Baby pictures are so
embarrassing.
Noogie convention!
Baa! What's up with Nate?

NATE WRIGHT: SUPER SCOUT!

I'll be honest: I used to think scouting was for dorks. But that was before Francis and Teddy convinced me to join their Timber Scout troop. **NOW** I know the truth: *SCOUTS ROCK!* For one thing, you get to wear an awesome uniform!

I LOVE your beret!

Plus, being a scout means going on overnight camping trips. That's always a blast, except for the time Dad came along as a parent volunteer. (Two words: **NEVER AGAIN!**)

Look at the squirrel, kids!

Dad, that's a SKUNK!

Scouting isn't free, though, so sometimes we do fund-raisers to earn money for our troop. Here's the problem: when you're trying to sell butt-ugly wall hangings of kittens and unicorns, you get a lot of doors slammed in your face.

You want me to buy **THAT?**

But it'll be worth it. Because guess what the grand prize is for the scout who raises the most money? (*HINT:* my old one is at the bottom of a swamp.)

It won't be easy. My main competitor, who's good at **EVERYTHING**, is probably a great salesman. I'll add that to the list of things I hate about him.

mystery rival

Want to know what happens? Here's how to find out:

Read **BIG NATE ON A ROLL!**

MY GREATEST ADVENTURE YET!

"Big Nate is funny, big time."
—Jeff Kinney, author of Diary of a Wimpy Kid

BIG NATE
ON A ROLL

Lincoln Peirce

Lincoln Peirce

is a cartoonist/writer and the author of the *New York Times* bestsellers *Big Nate: In a Class by Himself*, *Big Nate Strikes Again*, and the collections *Big Nate: From the Top* and *Big Nate: Out Loud*. He is also the creator of the comic strip *Big Nate*. It appears in two hundred and fifty U.S. newspapers and online daily at www.bignate.com. *Big Nate* was selected for *Horn Book Magazine*'s Fanfare List of Best Books of 2010 and BarnesandNoble.com's Top Ten. Also, *Big Nate* will be published in sixteen countries, including Brazil, Canada, China, the Czech Republic, France, Germany, Greece, Holland, Indonesia, Israel, Italy, Japan, Portugal, Spain, Taiwan, and Turkey, and will be translated into eighteen languages.

Check out Big Nate Island at www.poptropica.com. And link to www.bignatebooks.com for games, blogs, and more information about *Big Nate Boredom Buster* and the author, who lives with his wife and two children in Portland, Maine.

BIG NATE ON A ROLL AND
BIG NATE GOES FOR BROKE
ARE IN YOUR FUTURE!